ICE TIME

ICE TIME

David Trifunov

James Lorimer & Company Ltd., Publishers
Toronto

James Lorimer & Company Ltd., Publishers acknowledges the support of the Ontario Arts Council. We acknowledge the financial support of the Government of Canada through the Canada Book Fund for our publishing activities. We acknowledge the support of the Canada Council for the Arts which last year invested $24.3 million in writing and publishing throughout Canada. We acknowledge the Government of Ontario through the Ontario Media Development Corporation's Ontario Book Initiative.

Canada

The Canada Council | Le Conseil des Arts
for the Arts | du Canada

ONTARIO ARTS COUNCIL
CONSEIL DES ARTS DE L'ONTARIO

Cover image: Shutterstock
Cover design: Meredith Bangay

Library and Archives Canada Cataloguing in Publication
Trifunov, David, author
    Ice time / David Trifunov.

(Sports stories)
Issued in print and electronic formats.
ISBN 978-1-4594-0854-8 (pbk.).--ISBN 978-1-4594-0855-5 (bound).--
ISBN 978-1-4594-0856-2 (epub)

    1. Hockey stories, Canadian (English). I. Title. II. Series: Sports
stories (Toronto, Ont.)

PS8639.R535I24 2015   jC813'.6   C2014-908353-X
C2014-908354-8

James Lorimer & Company Ltd.,   Distributed in the United States by:
Publishers   Orca Book Publishers
317 Adelaide Street West, Suite 1002   P.O. Box 468
Toronto, ON, Canada   Custer, WA, USA
M5V 1P9   98240-0468
www.lorimer.ca

Printed and bound in Canada.
Manufactured by Marquis in Montmagny, Quebec in February 2015.
Job # 111636

To my wife, Erin, for her unwavering support,
love, and guidance.

CONTENTS

1 PLAYER INTRODUCTIONS

The dressing room door with the Edmonton Oilers logo on the front swings open. Paul Bidwell and his teammates emerge, waiting for their introduction to a legion of loyal fans scream-ing for them inside Edmonton's Rexall Place. Rock music blares. The Oilers tap their sticks against the rubber walkway and offer encouragement to each other in short bursts of chatter. Paul bends at the waist with his stick on his knees to stretch out his legs. It's going to be a tough, fast game.

Waiting for the Oilers on the other side of the arena is another group of young stars, from Colorado.

"C'mon, boys," one player shouts. "Let's go to work!"

The Oilers march confidently toward the ice. Arctic-blue and fiery-orange spotlights circle the rink. Fans scream, horns blare. As each player arrives at rinkside, he takes off like a shot around the back of the Edmonton net for warm-ups.

"Welcome to Edmonton's Rexall Place, hockey fans, for another night of Oilers' hockey. Tonight, the Colorado Avalanche are in the City of Champions. These are two of the NHL's best young teams, and we'll be sure to see plenty

of end-to-end, fast-paced hockey."

Paul and the Oilers are excited but not worried. Even when Colorado scores first, they don't panic.

"Taylor blasts down the right side and across centre ice," the play-by-play announcer says as Edmonton mounts an attack.

"Only Colorado's veteran goaltender is keeping them in this," the colour commentator adds.

"Taylor drops for Jordan. He doesn't keep it long. He sends a cross-ice pass to Smith on the opposite wing. Edmonton is really buzzing now. There's a furious pace to this game."

The television announcer's voice rises as he watches Edmonton cycle behind the Colorado net as if in a game of keep-away. Finally, Taylor spots a wide-open man.

"Bidwell's alone in front for a one-timer!"

Paul unleashes a rising slapshot that pings off the right post and into the net. He jumps in celebration. The game is tied, but it's no time to relax. The two sides trade chances all night until Edmonton prevails by the narrowest of margins over their rivals from the United States . . .

★★★

After the final puck hit the net, Paul let out a deep breath. It formed a frozen cloud above his head. He plopped down against the boards of the rink at Wilden Park in Saskatoon, not caring how cold the ice was under him. It was a tough game for one twelve-year-old kid to play by himself on an outdoor rink. He pushed his toque above his sweaty forehead to cool down.

Paul was a long way from the professionals playing in Edmonton or Colorado, but he loved to imagine himself skating alongside them. He looked around the neighbourhood as he thought about getting home. It was cold. It was dark. It was quiet. Paul had the ice to himself, again. He scanned the old, tiny houses up and down Elm Street for signs of life. The best he could see was glowing blue television sets through most of the windows. The Fairgrounds was one of Saskatoon's older neighbourhoods. Giant trees lined both sides of the street. Their branches touched at the top, making it feel like you were going through a tunnel as you walked down the road.

There were two schools a few blocks from each other. Paul went to St. James, but he usually played hockey in a park beside Wilden Elementary since it was a bigger rink with better boards. As Paul sat alone, one half of the ice was orange from the nearby street lights and the other half shone bright blue-white from the moon above. It was just enough for Paul to keep track of his shots. Most people would say he was playing in the dark, but Paul was pretty good at seeing what was happening. It hadn't snowed for days, either, so every crack was visible as he ripped around the rink, listening to the echo of his skates slicing along the blue-black ice. In his mind, he was just like the pros, but in his heart he knew his limits. Paul had never played on a real team before. He had never been coached on how to skate backward crossovers or learned the smallest details of a perfect team breakout. His hockey stick was wooden, not a cutting-edge composite like the ones most of his classmates used.

Still, he loved hockey more than anything.

There were floodlights around the rink, but they were shut off most weeknights. The shack to change into your skates was always locked, too. That was fine with Paul. Lights and a warm dressing room would only attract attention, and he'd rather master his skills alone. Instead, he changed into his boots outside in the dark. He tied his skate laces together, flung his skates over his shoulder, and headed for home.

Paul arrived to an empty house. He lived with his mom in a two-bedroom basement suite just a couple of blocks from the park. Because his mom worked shift work, Paul was often alone after school. If he needed anything, the lady upstairs was there to look out for him.

He almost never asked for anything.

"Did you have a good night?" Paul's mom asked when she finally got home.

"Great," he said as he hit the sack.

★★★

When the final bell rang the next day at school, Paul was still tired and his knees ached. He needed to put both hands on his desk to stand up. Yet, when his best friend, Vincent Friesen, asked him to play boot hockey, he was full of energy again.

"I've got practice, but not until late," Vincent said.

"Cool. Maybe you could show me your wrist shot," Paul replied.

They were halfway to Wilden when two older boys turned a corner in front of them. They had sticks over their shoulders and they were each wearing a different hockey jersey.

"Hey, Dillon, you guys want a game?" Vincent shouted at them.

The older boys went to high school with Vincent's brother. Dillon was wearing an old Saskatoon Impact sweater, the best triple-A team in the city.

"These guys look good," Paul whispered to Vincent.

"Don't worry. He didn't play for the Impact. That's his brother's jersey."

Paul was nervous, but he wasn't about to give up a chance to play with his friend. Vincent was always running off to games or practices after school. He was the best player on his peewee house-league team, the Wildcats.

"It's cool you can play for a while," Paul said as they hopped the boards. "I'm still mad you missed my birthday party."

Vincent and Paul used their hockey sticks to clear skiffs of snow from the ice. Asher and Dillon did the same across from them. They would play from side to side since there were just four of them. The rink was quiet. Only a few small kids were playing at the opposite end.

"That was the Davidson Tournament," Vincent said. "You just have to move your birthday. I can't miss that tourney."

Paul smirked. "Sure, I'll get right on that."

They bumped fists and started the game. With so much ice, there weren't many chances on goal. And they weren't wearing skates, just their boots. They played for half an hour, and the score was still only 3–3.

"Okay, next goal wins," Asher said. "Where's the ball?"

The bright orange hockey ball glowed even though it was half buried in a corner snowbank. Paul fished it out to restart play. He sent a perfect cross-ice pass to Vincent, who deked around Dillon and fired a wrist shot at Asher in goal. Dillon retreated fast. He stretched and deflected the ball with the blade of his stick.

"Not so fast!"

Paul ran furiously up the ice. He rejoined the play just in time to grab a rebound and coolly slotted the ball into the top-right corner of the net.

"Oh, yes! He shoots, he scores!" Paul shouted as Vincent raised his arms in shared celebration.

"What a perfect pass, just like I planned," Vincent said with a laugh. "Team Penguin wins again!"

Asher scrunched up his nose. "You think you're Crosby and Malkin? They're called the Penguins, not Team Penguin. You guys are weird."

Paul and Vincent just laughed. Team Penguin was their code. They were almost total opposites. Paul was tall and slender with brown eyes and dark hair. Paul's father was from the Caribbean country of Trinidad and Tobago, so Paul's skin was a bit darker than that of the other kids at school. Vincent was a bit shorter but also stronger. He had a fair complexion, with blond hair and blue eyes. They had been looking out for each other ever since Grade One.

"Too bad we couldn't play together for real," Vincent said as they packed up.

He didn't ask Paul to join very often, because he knew Paul and his mother couldn't afford the high fees and expensive equipment playing league hockey required. Paul's parents had divorced when he was younger, and his dad had moved back to Trinidad.

"Yeah, well, one day maybe," Paul said. "When we win the lottery. Then I can take you to Trinidad." He flicked a chunk of ice into a snowbank.

"That would be awesome," Vincent said, banging his stick on the ice. "You could buy me every Xbox game ever invented, and we could spend all day playing online and swimming in the ocean."

Paul turned to his friend with a big smile, smacking him on the chest.

"We'd have a seventy-inch TV, and those video-game chairs and headsets."

"But we'd have to come back in winter for hockey and pizza from Milano's every night," Vincent said.

Paul rubbed his stomach. "Oh, yeah, the Happy Hawaiian: ham, bacon, pineapple, and double cheese, with hot peppers. Extra large."

Vincent pretended to wipe drool from his chin.

"Hey, you wanna come over for supper? You could come to my practice."

"Nah. Thanks, though. My mom will be home at a normal time tonight."

They stepped off the ice and, without saying anything, started running. They were always competing, even if it was just to be first through the gate.

Paul's long legs meant he needed only a few strides, but Vincent was too strong and squeezed Paul to the side. "Ha, I win!"

"I let you have that one," Paul said as they crossed the street. "Hey, what are you doing this weekend?"

"We have a tournament. It should be a good one. I think we have a shot at winning it all."

"Nice," Paul said. "Bring me the gold medal on Monday."

2 MONDAY MORNING BLUES

Paul walked through the gate in the chain-link fence that surrounded St. James School fifteen minutes before the first bell rang. Jayson McDonough, Chad Wudrich, and Rudy Sandhu were standing outside the doors. All of them played for the Wildcats, and they were laughing about their tournament in Clavet that weekend. Paul decided just by looking at them that they were too happy for a Monday morning.

Jayson, the team's red-haired goaltender, waved when he saw Paul. "Paul, you should have seen it," he said. "We were awesome!"

Paul listened to Jayson talk about the "ridiculous" save he had made in the semifinal and the winning goal Vincent had scored in the final. Paul looked around, but Vincent wasn't anywhere. He tried to leave for class.

"Don't go anywhere until you hear about my save. You should have seen me dive across the net," Jayson said.

Paul paused and stayed to listen.

"The puck was at the left faceoff circle. One of the Cougars faked a shot, and then he passed it straight across my crease to a guy wide open at the far post. There were only thirty seconds left."

Paul was listening intently when he suddenly lurched to one side. Vincent had strolled up silently and banged into him with his shoulder, as if he was body checking Paul along the boards. "What's so exciting?"

"Here he is, our team captain, the In-Vince-able one," Jayson said as he continued with his story. "I was just about to tell them how you scored that amazing goal . . . after I'm done telling them about my awesome goaltending."

Chad and Rudy groaned, and Paul turned away. He studied Vincent's face. He'd known Vincent long enough to tell when something wasn't right. Vincent wasn't smiling, and he was quiet. Paul would have expected Vincent to take over the story. Instead Vincent, in a crouch, imitating a picture-perfect glove save, only watched Jayson.

"Anyway, I totally knew what he was doing. I could see his eyes," Jayson said.

The boys laughed and Rudy interrupted.

"You knew what he was doing? Yeah, sure you did! But you made the save. The Clavet kid couldn't believe it. He had a wide-open net. He put everything behind his shot."

Rudy stood out from the group and pretended he

was holding a hockey stick. He took a wild slapshot that forced him to drop down on one knee.

Vincent perked up. He had a small smile on his face but looked like he'd just woken up and was still very tired.

"Oh, now I remember," he said. "Jayson dove back across his net and got his blocker on the puck."

Paul looked back to Jayson, who had a confused look on his face.

"Great story, Vince, but it was a glove save," Jayson said.

"Yeah, right, but it won us the game."

"It got us into the final!" added Rudy.

"And then you won us the whole tournament," Chad said.

The three boys stood shoulder to shoulder. They started humming the words to "O Canada" as they unzipped their jackets to reveal gold medals hanging around their necks.

"The girls are going to love them," Chad said. "Vince, where's your medal?"

Paul looked over at his friend again as the second bell rang, telling everyone they had five minutes to get to class. Vincent was rubbing his temples and didn't answer.

"I guess we better get going," Paul said as they headed for the doors. "I would have loved to have been there to see that goal."

Vincent shrugged his shoulders. "It wasn't that big of a deal. I can barely remember it."

"The way Jayson talks, it was probably highlight of the night on TV," Paul said, a bit surprised at Vincent's shyness. He'd always known Vincent to be modest, but not this modest. Paul kept thinking there was more to the story, and he didn't know why Vincent wasn't sharing.

He trudged into the classroom behind Jayson, Chad, and Rudy, who were still beaming like their gold medals. Paul braced for a lousy day, and he was right.

Not only was it Monday morning, it felt like the coldest day of the year, and he had math first period, followed by French, and then language arts. When the lunch bell rang Paul expected to at least get more from Vincent about his goal.

He searched the halls and found Vincent at his locker.

"I gotta get home," Vincent said. "My head is killing me."

"You have a cold or something?" Paul asked.

"I dunno, maybe. Some guys on the team said they were getting sick. I should rest. I don't want to miss any games."

Vincent pulled on his jacket and grabbed his backpack. He closed his locker door quietly and left for home.

Paul spent most of the day by himself. He almost fell asleep in science, zoned out during history, and hardly noticed geography class beginning or ending. Instead of longitude and latitude, he thought about gold and silver medals.

When he finally got home, Paul dumped his book-bag onto a chair at the door and tossed his mitts onto the floor. He didn't care that his socks were still inside his boots as he kicked them onto the rubber mat. He regretted that decision right away. Paul's first step with his bare foot was right into a pool of melting snow.

"Ugh!" he shouted even though nobody was home to hear him. "How much worse can this day get?"

It was too cold, even for Paul, to play outside. He didn't feel like doing homework either, so he turned on the TV until his mom returned from work.

"How about you turn off the TV?" she suggested once she arrived home. "Let's get dinner ready together."

"Fine," Paul answered. "If you want."

He didn't say much throughout dinner. He just wanted to get back to the couch.

"How was school? What did you learn today?" Paul's mom asked after they'd finished eating.

That was a funny question, Paul thought. He'd learned that he missed a great weekend with his best friend, who had been playing hockey for two days straight.

"I learned that you remember the names of the Great Lakes by saying *HOMES*," he said, hoping that would be enough to stop her questions and get him back in front of the TV.

"Oh, I remember that," she said with a smile. "Do you remember what the *E* stands for? That was the one I always forgot."

"Erie," Paul said.

He didn't make eye contact with her as he pushed his fork around an empty plate. He leaned his head onto his other hand, his elbow on the table.

"Huron, Ontario, Michigan, Erie, and Superior. *HOMES*," he muttered.

Paul watched her and braced for a lecture. He knew he was being stubborn and that he wouldn't get away with it. Whenever she was unhappy with Paul, she let him know it.

"Yeah, that's it," she said softly and got to her feet. "Why don't you go do your homework in your room? I'll clean the kitchen."

Paul didn't move. He looked up slowly. He preferred when his mom got mad, because at least then he knew what she was thinking.

"I'm mad, you know," he said, finally.

"I know," she said. "I'm your mother. I always know when you're upset. Tell me why."

He slumped back onto his chair and she sat down again instead of washing dishes.

"Vincent was in Clavet this weekend with the Wildcats," he said. "They won the whole tournament. I wish I had been there."

Paul knew what she was going to say. They'd had

this conversation many times before, and it always ended the same way: maybe next year.

"You know we can't afford that right now," she said. "We're just getting our feet under us. Maybe we can talk about it next fall."

He didn't answer. She was right, of course, but that didn't make it any better.

"But you said this new job would pay you better." His mom had started working as a dispatcher with the police department, answering 911 calls. The pay was better than at some of her previous jobs, but because she had just started, she worked strange hours.

"I have to pay my dues," his mother said. "I should be getting more regular hours soon, hopefully."

Paul slid off his chair and shuffled toward his bedroom, thinking about Vincent's game-winning goal and those gold medals.

"Okay, fine. I'll just go to my room and wait until next fall."

3 RECESS ROUGHING

St. James was an old school with two entrances: the big, double doors for parents and visitors at the front, and a back door into a lobby — the "mud room" — where students could change their winter boots for school shoes. In the centre of the mud room was an old steel drum to hold hockey sticks for games of boot hockey at recess or noon hour. Like they did most days, the boys swallowed their lunches quickly as they half ran, half walked the halls to grab their sticks. Jayson led the way in the race to be first onto the ice, peeking around corners and looking out for the vice-principal. If the vice-principal spotted them running in the halls, he'd send them back to their classroom and make them walk back. It would cost them valuable minutes.

The small group of Grade Seven boys made it in near-record time and scattered to the racks to put on their boots and grab their sticks.

Paul's Sher-Wood — a wooden hockey stick his teachers said they had used when they were his age

— was always the easiest to find. It stood out among the Reeboks, Warriors, and CCMs that glittered under the lights. They had names like Ultimate, Thunderbolt, and Firestorm.

Paul was used to playing with a wooden stick by now, and he grabbed it eagerly as he pushed open the mud-room doors and the boys spilled into the wintry outdoors. After about ten minutes of shooting the ball around, they divided into teams for a game.

"Sticks in the middle," Chad yelled as kids from different grades gathered. He tossed one stick left, then another right.

Paul looked around at his team with confidence. They had Jayson in goal and Tracey Evans playing left wing. She was on the triple-A girls' team and was one of the best players in school. Paul was about to ask where Vincent was when the game began.

The action started quickly and before the game was five minutes old, Paul's team was leading 3–1. He added two assists as the lead increased to 5–2. Still, he wanted a goal, and got his chance just as lunch ended. The hockey ball bounded to him in his own zone. Paul faked like he was going to swipe it from danger. Instead, he dragged it to his right and fed a pass across to Tracey.

Paul ran up the right side of the ice as Tracey deked out several boys along the left boards. She moved into position near the centre of the ice and, without looking, fed a pass to Paul at the far post. He settled the skittering ball and snapped home a quick wrist shot through the goalie's legs.

Paul raised his arms. "Yeah! What a pass, Trace!"

She shuffled over to Paul. "That's how you do it."

Tracey gave him a high-five, then a tap on the head.

Chad dropped his stick and looked around at his teammates. "Can't anybody on this team play defence?"

"She deked you out, too," Jayson said from his goal crease. "I saw the whole thing!"

Paul's team was guaranteed victory with just a few minutes left in the break. He imagined digging through his desk and bringing out the Stanley Cup toy he had pulled from a cereal box last year. It had an Oilers logo on the front. He would parade that around the classroom, reminding everyone who had won the game at lunch.

"You guys better pull your goalie," Paul yelled. "You're going to have to hear us celebrate all afternoon!"

"Let's keep playing until the second bell!" Chad shouted back. "There's still time."

Paul thought Chad looked more agitated than he normally did as he grabbed the ball for a faceoff at centre ice. "C'mon you guys, let's go!" he called. "Don't let it end like this!"

Chad won the faceoff and dumped the ball into Paul's corner of the rink. He ran hard up the ice. Paul collected the ball coolly to shoot it down the ice. Just as he took the shot, though, Chad jumped into the way and extended his Thunderbolt. Their sticks collided and Chad's smashed into two pieces.

Crack!

"Hey!" Chad screamed. "My stick!"

He was left holding the top half as the blade went skidding across the rink and into a corner. Everyone on the ice stopped and turned to look at what had happened. Even the Grade Three kids playing tag outside the rink heard them and peered over the boards.

"Get that old wooden piece of junk out of here!" Chad yelled at Paul. "You owe me $140!"

He stepped closer to Paul, throwing what little he had left of the hockey stick along the ice at Paul's feet. They stood nose to nose.

"It was an accident," Paul said, trying to sound more confident than he felt. He wasn't exactly sure what had happened.

"Are they going to drop their gloves?" someone shouted.

Paul swallowed hard; he hoped Chad wouldn't go that far. He relaxed when Tracey stepped between them.

"Now, boys," she said as she adjusted Chad's toque over his ears and zipped his winter coat right to his chin. "You're going to catch a cold if you keep your jacket open like this, Chad. C'mon, Paul, we need to get to class."

Paul watched Chad's face turn bright red. He always thought Chad was extra nice to Tracey because he really liked her, and now he knew he was right. Chad stomped off the rink and into the school.

"Guess that wooden stick was a good idea," Tracey said as the second bell rang.

Paul was still a little dazed as he tossed his stick into the barrel and changed into his shoes. Chad was already sitting at his desk when everyone trooped into the classroom.

"I wasn't kidding, Paul," Chad said with a raised voice. "You have to buy me a new stick. You owe me, like, a hundred bucks."

While Paul avoided the spotlight, Chad loved attention. He had just moved into the area the summer before, and Paul hadn't really gotten to know him. Paul was trying to think of something to say when their teacher, Mr. Fontaine, came into the room and tossed his books onto his desk. He grabbed a dry-erase marker from the ledge and wrote "VOLCANOES" in bold, red letters across the board.

"Who owes you a hundred bucks?" he asked. "I want a hundred bucks."

The class laughed and looked at Chad and Paul. Both boys stared straight ahead. Mr. Fontaine told everyone to open their science textbooks to chapter nine, "Earth's Changing Surface." As he read about fault lines and earthquakes, Paul thought about what he would say to Chad.

There was no way he would pay Chad for the broken

stick. Those sticks were light and flexible, but they broke easily. It wasn't his fault, Paul decided. Besides, the only thing Paul had worth that much money might be his copy of *The Hockey News* magazine about the Chicago Blackhawks' Stanley Cup championship. The magazine, a gift from his grandmother, was a collector's edition. When Paul had brought it into school after his birthday, some kids in class said it would be worth plenty of money someday.

Paul wanted the clock to slow down, but the hands raced to 3:15 and the final bell. He kept his head down as he moved through the crowded hallways to his locker. *Phew, made it*, he thought, but he nearly fell over when someone clapped him on the shoulder.

"Hey," a voice boomed. Paul turned slowly and saw Vincent standing there, grinning.

"You scared me," Paul said. "I thought you were Chad."

"Why, did you think he was here to collect?"

"That's real funny, Vince," Paul grumbled. "Hey, how did you know about me breaking Chad's stick? I haven't seen you all day. How are you feeling?"

Paul put on his winter coat and stuffed books into his backpack as the two friends headed for the mud room.

"I'm better. Just a little headache. And don't worry about Chad. He knows we're friends, so he told me all about it, like I was going to handle it or something.

I just calmed him down. He has, like, eight of those sticks. He's always bragging about how much they cost, but he keeps changing the price. His dad buys them in jumbo packs."

Paul felt the tension slide off his back. He closed his eyes tightly and sighed. Ever since Grade One, when Paul moved to St. James School from across the city, Vincent had been helping him. Paul was shy by nature, and he felt a little different than his classmates. On Paul's first day at his new school, some of the kids asked him why his skin was so dark. To make him feel welcome, their teacher would pair Paul with Vincent — who was popular even then — for assignments and games. It worked. Vincent had had Paul's back ever since.

"Thanks, dude. I didn't want to have to talk to him about it. He doesn't want the money, right?" Paul asked.

Vincent laughed as he handed Paul his hockey stick from the barrel. They stopped to let some Grade One kids run past them on their way to the school bus.

"Do you think Chad needs money? Besides, those sticks aren't even close to $140," Vincent said. "I was serious about the jumbo packs, man. You can buy eight at once."

Paul managed something that resembled a laugh as he put on his boots.

"I've got early practice," Vincent said, "so I have to bolt for home."

Paul opened the door so Vincent could walk out

first. Paul was surprised to see Vincent immediately shield his eyes with his hand.

"You need sunglasses? It's not that bright out."

Vincent groaned. Paul wasn't sure what to do as Vincent gathered himself. He watched as Vincent stood still for a few seconds before he started walking toward the gate.

"Do you need help?" Paul asked, following along.

For the second day in a row, Vincent hadn't seemed himself. He had been forgetting simple things, too. Vincent said taking a half day away on Monday had helped him, but Paul wasn't sure anymore.

"You're never in this much of a rush to get home," Paul said. "Hey, did you remember your science textbook? You need to start studying for the unit test."

Vincent reached with his left hand to his shoulder, like he was about to take off his backpack and look for the book.

"Yeah, I'm pretty sure it's there," he said.

The distance between the two boys increased as they headed home in different directions. Paul stopped suddenly.

"All right, then, but maybe you should go see a doctor!" Paul shouted.

Vincent turned to face him, walking backwards. He cupped his hands over his mouth and yelled, "Not me, I'm In-Vince-able!"

4 SICK DAY

Paul arrived at school on Wednesday morning eager to hear how Vincent's practice had gone the night before. He loved to hear about the drills and strategies the Wildcats used, but Vincent was not in class. As Paul sat at his desk, Mr. Fontaine appeared from the hallway with a woman nobody recognized. She took a blue marker from the ledge of the whiteboard and wrote "Mononucleosis."

"This is Ms. Nadolny," Mr. Fontaine said. "She's a public health nurse."

Under *mononucleosis*, Ms. Nadolny wrote: "white tonsils, swollen lymph nodes in neck/armpits, rash." Finally, in big, bold letters, she wrote "WASH YOUR HANDS," and turned toward the class.

"Mono is very contagious," she began. "It can spread on hockey teams, for example, when players share water bottles. It might feel like the flu, but it's different. Don't share cups, and don't share gum."

The kids all said "Ewww" at once.

Yuck, who would share gum? Paul thought.

"I'm here to tell you how to avoid mono and what to do if you think you have it," Ms. Nadolny added as she passed out pamphlets. "It seems a hockey team some of your classmates play for was hit with mono. Six cases, if we're counting right, in a couple of schools."

The Wildcats picked up more than gold medals in Clavet, Paul realized. He looked over the glossy pamphlet. It told him anyone with mono could be home for at least two weeks, and maybe even a month. Vincent must have it, too, Paul decided.

"Some of you might know it as the 'kissing disease,'" Ms. Nadolny said as she returned to the front of the class.

A few kids snickered.

"Hey, Chad, you guys should just use high-fives to celebrate your goals," Tracey said.

Everyone burst out laughing. Even Mr. Fontaine and the nurse were smiling. Chad just scowled as they learned about good hygiene.

The rest of the morning was quiet; there weren't enough players for noon-hour hockey, either. Paul and a couple of other kids shot on Jayson in net, but even he wasn't interested. Paul flipped a weak wrist shot over Jayson's glove hand. He didn't even move.

"Nice shot," Jayson said sadly.

Paul walked toward the goaltender, and they stood in silence for a few minutes, watching as the younger kids took over the rink. Jayson used his stick to scratch caked-on snow away from the ice. It seemed to Paul that he was in a different world.

"There was nobody at practice last night," Jayson said. "There's no way we can win the championship unless we start getting better really soon. Everyone seemed fine on the weekend, and then all of a sudden, we're all sick. We were in first place."

He flipped a small block of snow at the boards. It exploded into a white haze.

"I guess Vincent has it, too," Paul said.

Jayson nodded. "I guess. He wasn't at practice. Coach told everyone to stay home if they felt sick, even parents."

The bell sounded to end the lunch hour. The boys lumbered into the mud room.

"We're going to forfeit our game this week and maybe next week if we can't get at least ten healthy players. There were only eight at practice."

Jayson lifted his goalie stick into the barrel like it was made of rock. He didn't even notice that the big goalie paddle was jutting out at an awkward angle.

Paul pushed Jayson's stick into the barrel for him. It made a loud *thunk*.

"You guys all have mono. That's crazy."

"Not all mono," he said. "A couple of guys have a bad flu. We had a couple of injuries before the tournament, too, and one guy got hurt in the first game. Everything went wrong so fast."

They didn't talk as they stopped at Paul's locker. They were both headed to science class for a test. Paul shrugged. "It's amazing you won that whole tournament."

"We thought it was good we could win that way," Jayson responded as they headed for their desks. "I guess we were wrong."

As the clock finally hit 3:15 and dismissal, Mr. Fontaine asked for volunteers to take homework to their sick classmates.

"Just leave it in the mailbox if you don't want to go inside," he suggested.

Paul grabbed work for Vincent and headed to his house. He was surprised to see Vincent's mother home early when he knocked on their door.

"Come on in, Paul. Vincent isn't supposed to have visitors, but you can stay for a couple of minutes."

"We learned all about mono in class," Paul said. "I won't get near him, I promise."

She led Paul down the hallway to Vincent's room, speaking softly as she went.

"Vincent doesn't have mono, Paul," she said. "We didn't even realize he had been injured, but he was tripped in the final game at the tournament. He has a concussion."

Paul's jaw dropped. He stared at her in disbelief.

He'd heard TV commentators talk about how dangerous concussions could be and how some players never recovered. Vincent's mom opened his bedroom door slowly. It was almost totally dark, but Vincent was awake.

"Geez, what happened?" Paul asked as he stepped into the room.

Vincent was lying on his bed, staring at the ceiling. "Hey, Paul, what are you doing here?"

Paul sat down in a chair in the corner of Vincent's room. He dropped his backpack and undid his jacket. "I brought your homework. I thought you had mono."

Vincent sat up slowly. "Nah, my dad talked to Coach last night. He told me some guys had it, but not me. I think this is worse, though."

Paul fished out Vincent's books from the backpack and placed them on the dresser.

"You should have told me at school. I thought something was weird."

Vincent reached for a water glass beside his bed. He took a long swig.

"I didn't know until last night. It probably happened when I slid into the boards during the championship game in Clavet."

Paul ran a hand over his head. It felt like he suddenly had a headache just listening to Vincent's story.

"I was skating hard down the wing and tried to get around a defenceman," Vincent added. "I guess our skates got tangled."

"That's brutal," Paul said. "I hope he got a penalty, at least."

"Of course not. The refs never call penalties for me. I kept playing, but I started getting headaches later."

He huffed a little. Paul stood and shuffled around the room anxiously.

"Mr. Fontaine gave you the science test to write at home," Paul said, "since it was open-book anyway."

Vincent laughed a little. "You could probably take that back. I'm not allowed to read or write for a couple days."

Paul decided he needed to sit down again.

"Will you be at school tomorrow? It's Thursday, so it's our easy day — gym, art, and social studies in the afternoon."

It was Vincent's turn to stand. He went to the window and opened the curtains a little.

"I won't be back until Monday if the headaches go away. But the doctor said I can't play any sports for at least a month."

He walked over to his Xbox and quickly and noisily crammed all the games and controllers into an empty box without trying to organize the cords or put the right games into the proper boxes.

"No video games, either, I guess," Paul said.

Vincent gathered some hockey magazines next and put them away.

"I won't be using any of this stuff for a while," he said. "No TV. No hockey. No reading."

He sat back down on the edge of his bed and sighed.

"This was going to be a great season."

"How did the doctor know it's a concussion?" Paul asked.

Vincent stretched out on the bed. "I went with my dad to the walk-in clinic when that headache got worse. The doctor checked me for strep throat. Then she asked me why I was squinting. She did a bunch of strange tests. I had to close my eyes and touch my finger to my nose. She even asked me math questions.

"I was having trouble remembering details about the tournament," said Vincent.

Paul was shocked, but he didn't want to show it. He wanted to stay cool and calm, to keep Vincent's spirits high. His friend sometimes forgot about science tests, but he never had any trouble remembering what went on during a hockey game. It made Paul really worried.

"When the doctor heard I had headaches and felt sick to my stomach," Vincent continued, "she said it probably was a concussion."

"I hate headaches," Paul said. "It would be terrible having them all the time."

"It's better in the morning, but worse in the afternoon," said Vincent. "Sometimes I feel okay, too, which is why I didn't tell anyone."

The boys sat in silence for a while. Paul kept thinking about what it would be like to give up hockey.

"If I get better fast enough, I might be back for playoffs," Vincent said finally, "unless we miss them."

Paul wasn't sure what would make Vincent feel better. He wanted to sound encouraging. "Hey, this won't last. You'll be back in no time."

"Let's hope so, Dr. Bidwell," Vincent said as he fished another Xbox game from under a pile of clothes. He tossed the game at the others and flung the clothes at his laundry hamper. "I was so close to making the rep team this year. I thought winning a championship would mean the coaches would notice me for next season."

Paul couldn't remember the last time he had seen Vincent so angry. He was sure Vincent was the best hockey player he had ever seen. If there was anyone who could play rep hockey, it was Vincent. When their class had a skating party before Christmas, Vincent was so fast both forward and backward it made Paul jealous. He loved watching his friend skate through the little kids on the ice. When the boys raced from blue line to blue line, Vincent won by a mile.

He didn't get a chance to cheer Vincent up. Vincent's mother appeared at the open door, and Paul stood to leave.

"Hey, Paul," Vincent said, "if you're not doing anything Friday, do you want to play some hockey with the Wildcats?"

Paul smiled. "I wish."

Paul gazed out his kitchen window at the dark Saskatoon night. He had decided it was too cold to play outside.

5 DARK KNIGHT

Plus, the Oilers' game was on TV in forty-five minutes. He'd have plenty of time to finish his homework before the game started.

He opened his binder, took out some scrap papers he didn't need, and tossed them into the recycling bin. He studied his notes and looked at his assignment sheet for social studies: *Read chapter three, "Canada's Neighbours."*

Paul started to learn all about issues that affected Pacific Rim countries, and decided to write a short essay about how hockey played a key role in Canadian–Russian relations. He'd just read all about the 1972 Summit Series in the library at school a few weeks ago, so he breezed through his homework faster than he had expected to. Paul looked over at the clock on the microwave again. There was still fifteen minutes until game time.

He returned to the living room and flopped onto the couch. Paul stared straight up at the ceiling. He listened to the endless drone on the television about something he didn't have much interest in, and then decided he wanted to see if it had warmed up outside.

Paul opened the door and stretched out his hand. He decided it really wasn't that cold so he stepped back in, quickly dressed, and headed the few blocks toward the rink.

He went through his usual routine. He put in a few laps making only right turns, because he was better at skating in that direction. He could go pretty fast, but once he tried left turns he felt unsteady and clumsy. Then he tried skating backward. No matter how hard he pushed, he just didn't get very far very fast. Next he dumped three pucks from his pockets and started taking some wrist shots on goal. He stood far back from the net, about where he thought the blue line would be in a real rink. He couldn't see very well, but that was making him more accurate.

Three pucks and three goals. Next he moved to slapshots.

Whack!

His first attempt sailed high over the boards.

"Oh, great."

He hoped the puck wasn't buried in a snowbank. Paul's second and third shots were better.

Ching! Ching!

Both found the steel mesh.

"Hey, Vincent! You should be at home, resting," a voice called.

Paul jumped a little. He looked over at the boards to see someone watching him. Paul didn't answer right away.

"You're just going to make it worse," the voice said again.

Paul strained to see who it was. He was a bit nervous but skated to the boards. It was just a kid, like him.

"Oh, I thought you were Vincent Friesen. Sorry, didn't mean to scare you," the boy said. "What are you doing out here alone at night?"

"I was just shooting on net," Paul said. "Vincent lives down the street. I could take you there, if you want."

The boy shook his head. "Thanks, I know where he lives. Hey, aren't you cold?"

Paul looked down at his hoodie and track pants. He shrugged his shoulders. "Not if I keep skating. Well, I get a little cold, but I don't mind."

"You're brave."

Paul thought he looked familiar, but he couldn't figure out from where.

"You must play hockey with Vincent," Paul said, finally.

"Yeah, on the Wildcats," the boy said. "Do you go to school with him? I thought you were him out here. That's why I shouted at you. I couldn't believe he could be out here because of his concussion."

The boy made his way to a gate in the fence. He leaned on the boards under a street light.

"I'm Carter Provost. My dad coaches the Wildcats," he said. "I was walking to Vincent's house to get warm." He pointed in the other direction. "My dad's car ran out of gas. He's walking to the station and will pick me up at Vincent's place. It's lucky we ran out of gas so close to where he lives."

"Oh," Paul said. "I go to school with Vincent. I know all about your team."

"Oh, yeah. Did you get a lesson in school about mono? We did. My dad and I were just coming back from an emergency team meeting. We might have to forfeit, like, three games. Maybe more."

Carter's nose was running and his face was bright red. He was covered head to toe by a parka, scarf, toque, and big leather mitts. He shuffled from side to side and banged his boots together, like he was trying to get the circulation going again in his toes, and then wiped his nose with a glove.

"Yeah, we got the mono lecture, too," Paul said, finally.

"It's the craziest thing," Carter said. "We're either sick or injured. My dad says he's never had this happen in twenty years of coaching. We had seventeen players; now we have eight or nine, if we're lucky."

Carter started to jump in place. "We don't have enough to play right now. We were in first place, but who knows now. Do you play for the triple-A team? Aren't you guys supposed to be in Regina this weekend?"

Paul smiled at the idea. "No. I don't play on a team. I just come out here by myself."

Carter's expression quickly turned from gloomy to goofy. He raised his hand to stop Paul from talking. He had a big smile on his face.

"Hold on — you're not on a team?" Carter's face glowed. "Did I hear that right? And you live in this area?" He pushed his toque off his forehead to expose his ears. "Do you realize that if we don't find another neighbourhood kid for the Wildcats, and soon, we are going to forfeit our next few games and miss playoffs?"

Paul smiled back, although he wasn't sure why. "Yeah, I guess so. That's what I heard, anyway, but I'm not sure what I can do about that." Paul shrugged.

"I do," Carter said. "You're the newest member of the Wildcats."

★★★

When Paul got home, he flopped onto the couch and turned on the hockey game for the start of the second period. He could barely concentrate. Colorado went on to beat the Oilers, but that wasn't why he had trouble sleeping later. He tossed and turned. He flipped his pillow. Then, once he did fall asleep, all he did was dream about playing for the Wildcats. Sometimes he scored the winning goal. Other times he searched and searched, but couldn't find his equipment.

When morning arrived, he stumbled into the bathroom and looked into the mirror. His eyes were red and his hair was a mess. Paul splashed cold water onto his face.

He didn't like the part of his dream about not having the proper gear; it felt too real. He didn't have hockey equipment — just beat-up skates and some wooden sticks. That's what made Carter's offer to play for the Wildcats that much harder to turn down. Paul wanted to play more than anything.

He had told Carter the night before he couldn't play. Carter didn't seem to care. He wanted Paul to think about it more and talk with the coach. The boys agreed to meet the next morning at the outdoor rink. After breakfast, Paul put on long underwear under his jeans, a sweatshirt, and his puffy winter jacket. He pulled on a toque and stepped outside. He knew it was going to be especially cold in the morning.

Paul was amazed to see Carter at the rink.

"Hey, where's your stick? Good thing I brought two."

"I didn't think you wanted to play," Paul said as he accepted a shiny Warrior stick.

They passed the puck back and forth without saying much. Finally, Carter snapped the puck into the net and walked over to Paul.

"So, what do you think about joining our team?"

"Like I said, I don't have any equipment, and my

mom just started a new job. Plus, she works shifts, so I wouldn't be able to get rides to games or practices."

He hadn't even talked to his mom about money, either. She'd worked late the night before and had still been sleeping when he woke up.

"I totally get it, but that's not what I asked. Do you want to play with the Wildcats?"

Paul was surprised. Carter sounded like an adult. "Well, yeah, I guess," Paul said. "I mean, if I could, I'd love to play."

"Okay, great. That's all I need to hear. Come with me."

Paul realized Carter wasn't going to take no for an answer. "All right, if it makes you feel better. But I don't think there's anything you can do."

6 GEARING UP

Carter interrupted Paul before he could say anything else.

"If you want to play, we're going to find a way for you to play. We really need help, and I have a good feeling about you. We're going to my place."

The boys walked to Carter's house, talking about their favourite players and teams. They traded stories about their schools and teachers. When they arrived at Carter's, Paul stood in awe. It was a huge brick home with a bright red door and a three-car garage. Tall evergreen trees stood in the front yard. A hockey net at the side of the driveway had a piece of wood covering its front. Its four corners were cut out, and so was the five-hole. It was nearly black from all the puck marks.

Parked in the driveway was an old car with a dent in the bumper and red tape over one tail light. Paul thought it looked out of place.

"Dad calls it his 'beater,'" Carter said. "He says why slide around on the snowy streets in a nice car? I think the gas gauge is broken, because he ran out of gas twice this month."

Paul smiled. If it wasn't for that old car, Carter never would have spotted him on the rink. Carter flipped open a small grey box at the side of the garage and pressed four numbers. The door lurched to life, rising to reveal a pristine blue sports sedan, a pickup, and what looked like a motorcycle underneath a tarp.

Carter walked to the back of the garage, still talking, but Paul was looking at the tarp.

"Nice, a motorcycle. Cool."

"Yeah, it's a Harley-Davidson. A Fat Boy," Carter said.

Paul followed Carter to a storage locker big enough to stand in without ducking. Carter opened the right door just a crack. "Help me with this."

He struggled to free an empty CCM hockey bag from the locker while keeping two baseball bats, fishing nets, and cross-country skis — with poles — from falling. Paul grabbed the hockey bag and plunked it onto a workbench. Carter returned to the locker and shuffled past a couple of golf bags. A basketball rolled along the floor and wedged itself under the front bumper of the shiny car behind them.

Carter turned back again holding a pair of shin pads. He stuffed them into the hockey bag. He grabbed some hockey pants and shoulder pads from the locker, too. He took a plastic shopping bag from a hook and pulled out two pairs of plain black socks and a white jersey. He placed them on top of the other gear. "Here. This is for you."

Paul wasn't paying attention. He was too busy studying the equipment.

"What do you mean, 'for me'?"

"These are yours now. We still need to find you a helmet, gloves, and some other stuff, but I think that will be easy."

Paul looked back into the bag, stunned. The equipment was nearly new.

"I can have all this stuff?"

Carter was smiling and that made Paul a little embarrassed. Carter zipped up the bag and rolled it off the workbench onto the garage floor.

"Let's just say you can borrow it for as long as you need," Carter said as they walked out of the garage. "My dad's a hockey coach. Lots of times people just give us equipment to use however we want. And I have two older sisters who play. If you think you're stealing all our equipment, just wait until you see our basement. Have you ever thought about playing goalie?"

Paul stopped. "Uh, well . . ."

"Just kidding, just kidding," Carter said with a grin. "We don't need a goalie."

Carter invited Paul into his home to talk more about the team.

"I won't tell anyone if you don't, but those hockey

pants and shin pads belonged to my oldest sister before she outgrew them," Carter said. "She's way taller than me, and I don't fit into them, but they'll be perfect for you."

They went through a side door, leaving their shoes on a landing at the top of stairs. Carter carried the bag downstairs, letting it *clunk* off every step. Paul couldn't get over how warm the house was. It smelled like pine trees and clean laundry. The basement was fully furnished. It had wood-panelled walls with team photos hanging in every available place. Trophies lined the shelves, with newspaper clippings framed or just taped to the wall. Paul could see still more hockey photos and newspaper stories bursting from albums scattered throughout the bookcases. There was an air-hockey table, couch, and TV. A PlayStation, two controllers, and a dozen games spilled everywhere. At the centre of the side wall were three large, framed pictures.

The first photo showed a little girl dressed in a green jersey, trying to balance on skates for her first hockey photo. Pictures of another girl and a little boy hung beside it.

"That's me and my sisters from our first hockey teams," Carter said. "My mom got them blown up like that."

Paul was still looking around when Carter dropped the hockey bag and unzipped it.

"You know how this stuff fits together?" Carter asked.

Paul tried to think of what to say. He didn't want

to admit he'd never worn a full set of equipment. He'd worn Vince's hockey gloves and a helmet a few times just to try them out, but he didn't like them. The gloves made his hands feel too bulky, and he didn't see very well from behind the cage of the helmet.

"I didn't think so," Carter said after Paul didn't answer. "Here are the shin pads. Tighten them so they don't droop, but not too low. You don't want them to stop you from skating."

Carter gave similar instructions for the shoulder pads and pants. He went and grabbed one of his dad's old helmets from behind the air-hockey table and plunked it onto Paul's head.

Paul stood in the basement feeling like a knight in heavy armour, ready for battle. "I don't know how I'm going to skate in all this gear."

"You'll get used to it," Carter replied.

Paul swished back and forth through the basement, pretending he was skating, when a girl suddenly appeared from upstairs. Paul froze mid-swish.

His head was down, so all he could see were her painted red toenails on the bottom step. He looked up slowly, humiliated that he was wearing hockey gear inside. He was even more embarrassed when he saw how pretty she was. She had long dark hair and light brown eyes. Her blue sweatshirt said "Saskatoon Swift Midget AAA Hockey" over a snow-white fox logo.

She looked at Paul and then over his shoulder to

her brother on the couch. "A little late for Halloween, isn't it? Hey, are those my old shin pads?"

"Can't you see we're busy, Faith? We're planning our championship strategy."

She chuckled as she went to the dryer to get some clothes.

"Oh, are we finally going to put a trophy of *yours* down here? I guess we'll have to put some of mine in storage to make room," Faith said as she turned to leave, her long legs taking the stairs two at a time.

"Agh!" Carter shouted and tossed a pillow at his sister — or at least in her general direction.

Paul enjoyed their teasing, and he guessed the siblings must have some interesting conversations when all three kids were in the same room. Paul finally felt comfortable enough to continue swishing back and forth. He returned to the couch, where Carter was thumbing through a cellphone.

"Who you calling?"

Carter showed him the screen. On the front was a blurry picture of Jayson. He was opening his mouth so wide it was like he was trying to eat the phone.

"I'll put him on speakerphone," Carter said. "We need to find you the rest of the equipment."

It rang a few times before a groggy-sounding voice answered.

"Hullo." Jayson's voice was unmistakable.

"Man, are you still asleep? It's 10:30 in the morning!"

Carter shouted. "I've been up for two hours trying to save our hockey team."

There was no response.

"Who is this?" an obviously sleepy Jayson asked, and both Carter and Paul cracked up.

"It's Carter and Paul Bidwell. Paul's the newest member of the Wildcats. He's going to save the season. You can thank us by bringing your extra helmet to Wilden Park in an hour — and bring a stick. We're going to play some boot hockey."

It took a while for Jayson to respond.

"I bet he thinks he's dreaming," Paul laughed.

A few more phone calls and Carter reached most of his teammates. He asked Matthew Yeo to bring hockey gloves.

"The guy is huge. He must grow an inch every week," Carter said. "He probably goes through two sets of equipment a season."

Every time Carter ended a call, Paul got a little more excited and nervous.

"All the healthy guys can be there," Carter said. "I know you go to school with a couple of them, but we have players from three or four other schools on our team. I just have one more phone call. I'm sure you know Chad."

Paul's stomach did an anxious flip as he remembered the last time he'd played with Chad.

"Yeah. I know him."

7 PAYING UP

Paul and Carter were first to arrive at Wilden Park on the clear, still-cold morning.

"You've got a wicked shot," Carter told Paul as he fed him passes from the corner. "You've missed only one or two. That's awesome."

Paul felt good swinging away at the net. Carter's passes were nearly perfect. But the best part was using one of Carter's Warrior hockey sticks. It was so light compared to his wooden sticks, and it flexed just enough to give his shots an extra pop.

"These sticks are amazing," Paul said as he pelted another puck off the inside post and into the wire mesh.

Carter was standing deep in the corner to the left of the goal. He passed pucks to Paul at the right wing, about where the hash marks would be if they'd been on an indoor rink with painted lines. Paul was a left-handed shot, so Carter put him in a position that might be found on a Wildcat power play.

"Sometimes it's tough to make this pass all the way

across the ice," Carter shouted as another puck skidded to Paul, "but if you can make this pass, you should be wide open there and have a wide-open net, too."

Paul could envision himself sneaking behind the defence for a back-door pass, and then slamming home a winning goal. But he also liked the idea of passing to a teammate, so he asked Carter to switch places. The boys gathered about a dozen pucks from around the rink and set up so Carter could shoot on net.

The middle part of the ice was a bit rough with some packed snow. It meant Paul had to lift the puck into the air so it landed where Carter could get a decent shot on bare ice. Paul realized quickly just how difficult it was. Carter had made the passing look easy.

Paul's first few attempts didn't go well. He didn't put enough power behind his passes. A few pucks didn't make it past the snow in the centre, or veered away completely.

"It's tricky," Carter said. "It needs to be powerful but on target. Don't be afraid to really hit these passes hard."

Paul stopped worrying about messing up, and soon he was putting pucks right in front of Carter, who bashed a few into the net.

"Nice saucer pass, rookie," a voice over Paul's shoulder said.

He turned to see Jayson sitting on the boards,

watching. It was then that Jayson produced the helmet he'd been asked to bring with him. Soon, half a dozen other boys arrived, including Matthew with the extra gloves. The newest Wildcat now had everything he needed to play his first game.

"Thanks so much, you guys," Paul said.

He took off his mitts and slipped on the gloves. He grabbed his stick and flipped it around a bit. Sure enough, it felt odd. The armoured gloves felt to Paul like they were going to fall off his hands. At least with a bit of practice passing some pucks, they slowly started to feel better.

"I'm sure I could've found everything I needed somewhere, but this stuff is almost new," Paul said.

"It's no problem," Jayson said. "I'm going to be an all-star goalie in the NHL. I won't need this helmet."

Carter stepped toward Paul and looked over the helmet.

"Yeah, right," Carter said, checking the inside of the helmet to make sure all the padding was in place.

Paul was suddenly nervous with so many people relying on him. Yet they were all very friendly, which made him feel better. They spread out on the ice, shooting on net and passing pucks. They traded jokes, and talked about that epic Colorado–Edmonton game on TV.

Soon, they split into two teams and played some ball hockey. There were only nine boys at the rink, so

Jayson, Matthew, Carter, and Paul formed one team against the five others.

"It's okay," Carter said. "We can take you five on. This is my boy Paul's home rink. He's our secret weapon."

With Jayson in goal and Matthew playing defence, Paul and Carter were free to handle all the scoring chances for their team. Paul tried especially hard to impress his new friends, but the game stayed close for thirty minutes.

"Next goal wins," shouted Cody Hillier, who was clearly a defenceman.

Carter met Nathan Jenson at centre for a faceoff, to make sure the winning goal would be fair. Paul knew this was his final chance to show everyone he could help the team. He took off his gloves to cool his hands down, put them back on, and squeezed his stick. He kept sliding his gloves up and down looking for the best grip. He didn't want to mess up now.

Carter won the draw by scooting the puck between Nathan's legs. Paul knew that running on the clear ice through the middle of the rink was difficult, so he used the snow-covered right wing to get an advantage. He curled behind Carter, crossing from the left side, and sprinted down the boards. Carter saw what was happening and dumped the ball high into the air behind the defence.

Paul picked it up along the boards, cut hard into the centre of the ice, and deked around the goalie before sliding the ball into the empty net. He didn't even have to raise it. He just slammed it home. The ball made a loud *clang* as it hit the back bar.

"Oh, yeah! Look at this guy," Jayson shouted from behind the play. "He's going to rock!"

Most of the guys congratulated Paul as they packed up and headed for home. They told him they looked forward to seeing him on skates at practice in a couple of days. Paul, Carter, and Jayson were the last to leave. They leaned against the boards and talked about the next official practice on Monday night and what Paul should expect.

"Don't worry," Carter said. "My dad knows you're new to this. He'll make sure you understand the drills. It won't be too complicated, especially if there are only ten of us."

Paul took off his hat and wiped his brow.

"I'm glad I get two practices," he said. "I guess I have a lot more gear to pack home now."

He started to collect some of his things when Carter interrupted.

"I've got a question for you, Jay," he said. "Are you forgetting anyone else at your school who could play for us this year?"

"Oh, man," a smiling Jayson said. "Don't do that to me, Carter. I didn't think Paul was allowed to play, because of, you know, the money thing."

The boys immediately went quiet. Paul could see

Jayson's face turn red with embarrassment. He immediately tried to backtrack. He apologized three or four times in the space of a minute.

"I—I didn't mean to mention it. It just slipped out," he stammered.

Carter thumped Jayson on the back and looked over at Paul.

"Mr. Polite does it again," said Carter. "But if you know of any other amazing hockey players who are looking for something to do, let us know."

Paul could see Jayson's face was still red.

"It's okay, Jayson. You're right, anyway," Paul said. "It's just my mom and me, so paying for all that gear is tough. I'm happy to use whatever gear you have lying around so I can help out the team."

Paul had started to pack his equipment into a bag when a white truck pulled into the parking lot and Chad jumped out. Paul's heart sank.

"Hey, Chad," Jayson called. "Where've you been? Paul's gonna play for us. Now we don't have to forfeit any more games."

Chad walked slowly toward the boys. He didn't have a stick, and he was dressed in only a light jacket with no hat; he clearly wasn't going to play. He looked at Paul but didn't say anything.

"Seriously, Carter, *this* is your plan to save our season?" Chad said. "We should've had a team vote on this. I think we could have done better."

Paul was hurt, and he could see the other boys frown.

"No way is this going to work. He's never played real hockey, you know," Chad scoffed.

Carter stepped in front of Paul, and Jayson followed.

"That's not cool, Chad," Carter said. "It's not like you had any ideas of how to keep the team playing."

Chad turned to walk back to the truck, saying over his shoulder, "It doesn't matter. The season is over, anyway. We don't have a chance now. I'll probably go play for the Phantoms next season, anyway. Like my Dad said, 'What does a kid from the Bahamas or wherever know about hockey?'"

"You're going to quit just like that?" Carter shouted back. "That's cheap. You're going to leave us in a worse situation."

"And his dad is from Jamaica," Jayson added. "Get it right!"

Paul winced. He thought about telling them his dad was from Trinidad but decided against it. He just wanted them to stop shouting. "It's okay, guys. He's right, anyway. I have to prove myself on the ice."

Chad laughed and kept walking toward the truck. He looked back at the three boys before getting inside the pickup. "I hope you're making him pay registration, at least. This isn't some charity team."

They watched as the truck backed out of the parking lot. Nobody said anything right away, and Paul knew Chad was right about the money. The Wildcats had given him the extra equipment and made him feel like part of their team, already. Now he had to come up with the money. "I guess I better get home and talk to my mom."

8 PRACTISE LIKE YOU PLAY

Sunday was the one day Paul and his mom always spent together. They usually had a late breakfast, and there was always Sunday dinner with his grandmother. Paul was especially excited this time. He'd met the Wildcats, and the next day would dress in his "new" gear and skate with the team at a real practice. Jayson and Carter had even taken his side against Chad.

There was just one thing weighing on his mind: money. He had never played organized hockey because of the cost. His mother had offered to enroll him in indoor soccer, but it just wasn't the same. Now he had his chance to play hockey; he just had to pay the registration fees. Carter told him a season of house-league hockey was about $550, plus equipment and travel costs to tournaments. Because Paul was joining for just the last five weeks of the season, the cost would be only $100. There were no more tournaments, so he didn't have to worry about that.

He was making toast when his mom appeared in

the doorway of the kitchen from her bedroom. He had put plates on the table, with bowls on top. Knives and spoons rested on napkins, while glasses sat waiting for milk or orange juice. He had also poured her a cup of her favourite tea, orange pekoe. The butter, jam, and peanut butter were there for the toast, beside two boxes of cereal and two grapefruit halves. Sometimes she made pancakes on weekends, but Paul wanted to show her how independent he could be.

"Wow," his mom said as she entered the kitchen. "Thank you, Paul. This is such a nice treat, to have everything so nicely placed on the table. What's the special occasion? Mother's Day isn't until May."

Paul was about to answer when the toast popped. He grabbed and buttered it while it was still hot. He poured her some orange juice and held the chair for her, just like in the movies. Then he sat across from her, grabbed two pieces of toast from the stack at the centre of the table, and started to make his own breakfast.

"So, Mom," Paul began. "I went to Carter's house yesterday, and he loaned me a whole bunch of hockey gear for free. I just have to give it back when I'm finished with it."

He watched his mother slow her chewing as she listened. She had a look that told Paul she knew he was up to something.

"Oh, Paul," she said through her bite of peanut-butter toast. "I thought we talked about this. We agreed it was too difficult for you to play hockey this year. But if you wanted . . ."

He interrupted her but remained calm. "That was before I met the team," he said, opening the strawberry jam. "They're great, and they really need me. They're all expecting me at practice tomorrow."

She put down her tea. He knew she would want to talk to the coach, but everything had happened so quickly, he hadn't had a chance to speak with her first. She wanted to say something again, but Paul kept talking. He thought if she had the chance, she'd just say no.

"Carter said the registration fee would be less than half of what it is for a whole season. Way less," Paul said. "Plus, he thinks I'll qualify for something called Jump Start."

He produced the brochure Carter had given him. It said Jump Start helped kids in financial need pay their fees to play sports.

"It's for kids who want to play," he said, "but need some help."

His mother's expression softened. She walked over and gave him a big hug from behind as he sat in his chair.

"Aw, Mom," Paul said as he squirmed in her embrace.

"Okay, you can play, but I want to meet this coach."

Paul was so happy he jumped up and banged the table with his leg. The knives and spoons rattled, and a plate crashed into a glass.

"Really? That's wicked! Thanks, Mom. I'm going to call Coach right now and tell him he can bring over the registration forms!"

He ran from the room to find the cordless phone. Within the hour, Coach Provost was having a coffee in their kitchen, reassuring Paul's mom that her son was stepping into a welcoming, safe environment. Because it was a special situation, he promised to pick Paul up for games and practices.

"I am guaranteeing you that your son will have the best time of his life," Coach said. "My boys this season are really good hockey players, and they're all great kids."

Paul's mom fiddled with a pen. She looked at the registration form, the coach, and then her son.

"Isn't it too late to register?" she asked.

"We've gotten special permission. The league is letting us play with twelve, but we expected to have only ten or eleven players for a couple of weeks. That's why Paul is so important. Today I have only nine, but I'm hoping some kids start to get healthy this week."

Paul's mom clicked the pen open again. She signed her name and slid the form across the table to Coach. He folded it quickly and jammed it into his pocket.

"Yes!" Paul shouted.

★★★

Paul couldn't remember ever being so excited. After packing and repacking his borrowed equipment three times the night before, and then re-taping his hockey sticks, he barely slept. At school, every minute seemed like an hour. He ate something light after school and was waiting in the driveway when Coach and Carter arrived for practice.

Finally, Paul was at the rink, lugging his hockey bag through the arena doors just like he'd always dreamed of doing.

Carter looked back over his shoulder at Paul. "You ready for this?"

Paul stared at the Zamboni smoothing over the ice. "I'm ready."

He followed Carter into the dressing room where most of the Wildcats were already putting on their equipment.

"Hey, boys!" Carter yelled.

The Wildcats greeted Carter and Paul with a chorus of whoops and hollers.

"Hey, Paul!" Jayson shouted.

"What's up, rookie?" Nathan chimed in as he crossed the dressing room floor after tossing a water bottle into the recycling bin.

The room was nearly empty with so many players away, so Paul chose a space between Carter and Jayson when the door swung open again.

"Don't take my place!" Chad yelled as he dragged his equipment into the room.

"It's in this corner. That's my stall," he said, pointing to an empty section of the wall.

Paul stared in bewilderment. The room was almost empty. There was space enough for ten more players, and all four corners of the dressing room were empty.

The room went silent after that. Chad had a way of making everyone uncomfortable, Paul thought as he un-packed. But it wasn't going to ruin his good mood. He was too happy with how things were going. His heart was beating a mile a minute as he looked around the room to watch how others were putting on their gear.

It seemed every player had his own unique way of putting on his equipment. Paul started with his shoul-der and elbow pads. He then slipped on his hockey pants. He sat down again ready to put on his shin pads and skates. Paul bent over, but realized his shoulder pads were too bulky and it would be nearly impossible to get his shin pads and skates on after that. He looked around, a little embarrassed, and quickly took off his upper-body stuff so he could get his shin pads adjusted properly and his skates tied tightly.

Nobody seemed to notice. At least Carter — who was waiting to walk with him onto the ice — didn't say anything.

Paul took a deep breath, checked his helmet straps, and grabbed his sticks. Beyond the door was a real, honest-to-goodness hockey practice — his first. It was going to be amazing. He was expecting to see the

Wildcats — helmets off, like the pros do in warm-ups — flying around the ice with their hair blowing in the breeze. There would probably be whistles blowing and coaches yelling instructions.

He was wrong.

Most of the guys were taking a leisurely skate around the ice, some were stretching, and others were sitting on the bench waxing their sticks so they wouldn't get too much snow on their blades. Coach was in a corner, diagramming something on a whiteboard hanging from the glass.

All he could hear was the rink attendant shovelling snow beside the Zamboni. Still, he walked excitedly along the rubber pathway to the edge of the rink. There was the gate, the ice gleaming behind it. Paul had finally made it.

He took a deep breath, stepped onto the ice, and fell flat on his back.

9 HITTING THE ICE

The first thing Paul heard was Jayson's laugh. Paul was just steps from the arena door, lying on his back. The rest of the team slapped their sticks on the ice in applause. Paul was humiliated. He'd been on arena ice during school trips, but he had forgotten how different it was from outdoor rinks. Outside, the ice was almost never freshly flooded. The rink at Wilden Park often had a layer of hard-packed snow around the edges that slowed everything down. It had cracks and sometimes so many ruts that even playing hockey at all could be difficult. Paul fell plenty of times there, but it was usually because his skate blade caught a crevice, sending him sprawling.

"You okay?" Carter asked.

Paul had a choice. He could get up and pretend nothing had happened. Or he could walk back into the dressing room, take off his gear, and go home. Instead, he stood and took a huge bow. He bent deeply at the waist and tucked his arm under his stomach like he was

meeting the queen of England. All the Wildcats roared
with approval.

"Okay, boys, let's get it going," Coach said to calm
them down. "Let's have five minutes of free skate.
Everybody grab a puck, with two guys at every circle."

Paul had no idea what was going on, but he glided
over to the bench with the rest of the group, grabbed a
puck, and tried to look like he knew what he was doing.

"Come with me," Carter said, and they headed to
the opposite side of the rink.

The drill got their legs moving. Players skated
through a faceoff circle with a puck, stickhandling and
then kicking the puck from their skates to their sticks.
Paul wanted to throw his gloves and helmet over the
boards, but he knew he'd have to get used to them
eventually. At least, as the practice wore on, he started to
get used to the thick layer of padding and plastic.

Coach then blew his whistle and asked for everyone's attention. From there it was more drills for agility
and balance. They skated around the rink and kicked
their legs high and bent their knees. Sometimes Coach
dropped pylons for players to skate around. Paul felt
good going from left to right but was totally uncomfortable crossing his right leg over his left.

After that, Coach split them into three groups for
passing practice. At a station with Nathan and Carter,
Paul was on his knees with his back to them. He jumped
up, turned, and took a pass from Carter. He passed it

back to Nathan and then dropped down again. Paul had trouble receiving the first few passes; they came across the clean ice quicker than Paul anticipated. Carter put so much juice behind his passes they nearly knocked Paul's stick from his hands. After a while, though, he began to receive the passes properly.

Passing was easier. Paul felt like he knew where Nathan was without even looking at him.

Paul was feeling good when Coach skated over to watch. "Your passing is good, Paul, but let's talk about skating."

He blew his whistle and asked Carter to set up the one-puck horseshoe drill. Everyone cheered and formed two lines in opposite corners for a one-on-one scoring drill.

Paul watched the others hustle into place before he skated to the opposite end of the ice with Coach. They set up at the far blue line near the boards facing the goal line.

"Has anyone ever taught you how to skate, Paul?"

"Well, one of my uncles gave me some help, but I pretty much just watched what other kids did, and watched on TV, too," he answered.

"That's good," Coach replied. "You learn quickly, then. But I want you to start over."

"Starting over" sounded intimidating to Paul, but Coach was very positive. He began by teaching Paul the "sit position." Paul's skates were too close together;

they were supposed to be as wide as his shoulders. Coach asked Paul to pretend he was going to sit in a chair. Almost immediately Paul could feel his leg muscles start to burn.

"That deep knee bend gives you a lower centre of gravity," Coach said. "That means you can absorb any bumping on the ice and stay on your skates. It gives you good balance."

Paul's hands were too far back, too. Coach wanted Paul to think of his stick as a steering wheel.

"Keep your head up and your hands in front so you can take a pass," Coach shouted over Paul's blades schussing hard toward the end boards. "Keep two hands on the stick, and keep that stick on the ice."

For ten minutes all they did was skate from the blue line to the goal line and back. Then they skated from the blue line around the faceoff dots, both left and right.

"When I skate to the left, I feel really weak," Paul said as he wobbled around the red dot. "Like I'm going to fall over, or my skates are going to bump into each other."

Coach showed Paul how to keep his left skate ahead of his right, and to use his "steering wheel" to perform a tight curl around the faceoff dot then charge hard the other way.

"That felt better," Paul said after attempting it a few more times.

"Good," Coach answered. "Next time we'll work

on your crossovers, backwards skating, and transitions."

Sweat dripped into Paul's eyes, but he loved every second on the ice. He could feel himself getting better by the minute. Things started to click. He was feeling more confident, until a familiar voice interrupted the practice.

"What about the rest of us?" Chad yelled. "We have to work on our power play and our breakout."

Coach blew his whistle to gather the boys at centre ice. Paul could see Coach's face sour.

"Okay, that's enough," Coach said as he and Paul rejoined the group. "Maybe you should have joined us, Chad. Your stride needs work. Or don't you remember how difficult it is to master skating?"

Chad didn't say anything.

"There might be only ten or eleven of us on Friday night against the Panthers. If we're lucky, we might have twelve," Coach barked. "They might be low in the standings, but they'll probably have a full team, and we need to be ready."

The practice got a lot harder after that. They worked on cycling in the offensive zone, and neutral zone traps. They defended the slot, stretched their passes, backchecked, and forechecked. Paul was especially lost during something called the "three-on-two continuous drill" that helped the team break out from its zone. Three forwards carried the puck against two defencemen. After one attempt on goal by the forwards, the defencemen took over, passed the puck out of the zone, and the drill started all over again.

Paul played wing and had to skate hard down the boards. Sometimes he would shoot, and sometimes he would look for a rebound. Then, it was back in the other direction to start over. He felt like he was always trailing.

"Come on, Paul, keep those legs moving," Coach shouted over the roar of skate blades and echo of pucks against glass.

With barely enough players to run the drill, it meant everyone had to really be paying attention. Once or twice, Coach had to stop them so Paul could find his place. It took him two or three tries, but eventually he started to understand what was happening.

By the end of practice, Paul's head was still spinning. Some of the drills reminded him of his math homework, but he also felt proud to have learned so much so quickly.

"What did you think?" Carter asked him as they removed hockey tape from around their shin pads in the dressing room.

"It was amazing."

★★★

The next day, Paul was thrilled to see Vincent walking to school. Paul couldn't wait to tell him about practice.

"Vince! You're here," Paul said as they met on the street. "You feeling better?"

"Yeah, sort of," Vincent said quietly. "I'm still not feeling great, but at least I can go to school. I didn't think it was possible, but I missed the place." Vincent wasn't smiling.

"I thought if you were back at school, you'd be able to play hockey," Paul said.

They walked into the mud room. Paul dumped his hockey stick into the barrel. Vincent wasn't carrying anything except a small bookbag that didn't look like it had any books inside it.

"Getting back to school is only the beginning," Vincent told him. "If I can concentrate in class without getting a headache, I can come back tomorrow. If not, I have to stay home."

Paul's good mood disappeared "Man, that stinks."

"The doctor said I was doing better with the concentration tests, but I'm still having trouble sleeping. She won't let me start exercising for at least another week."

"A week? Wow, that's a long time," Paul said.

"Then I have to ride an exercise bike for a while," Vincent said as they arrived at the classroom. "If I'm not sick after that, then I can skate."

He had to be symptom free, which meant no nausea, no headaches, clear vision, good hearing, and lots of energy. Paul stood back to let Vincent go into class first.

"Go ahead," Paul said. "Everyone's been talking about you."

"I'm going the other way. I'm going to be doing my work in the library until I'm better. It's quieter."

Vincent glanced into the classroom and waved. Paul heard the shouts from inside and smiled.

"Hey, enough about me," Vincent said. "How was practice?"

Paul's face lit up. "It was so much fun. I wish you had been there. I needed you to explain that continuous drill."

Vincent patted Paul's shoulder. "Just wait until we show you the Oil Can drill. Now that's confusing."

Paul realized he'd been laughing and smiling almost the whole time they'd been talking. He tried to stop himself. He felt like he was bragging. It wasn't much use. He just kept smiling when Vincent took a step inside the classroom.

Everyone cheered, and the shouting didn't stop until Mr. Fontaine appeared from the teachers' lounge to start class.

"Vincent, good to see you up and around," the teacher said. "Paul, you joining us?"

"I'm coming. I was just talking to Vince about his hockey team."

Vincent stopped Paul before they parted ways. "You mean our team."

Paul smiled even wider. "Yeah, I guess so. *Our* team."

10 OVER THE BOARDS

Paul's second practice started right where his first practice had ended. It felt like they were on the ice for only minutes when the horn sounded to usher them off the ice for the next group. Paul wanted more time to master his skating. He was only beginning to skate faster going backward. The other stuff — penalty killing and five-on-five play — Paul was more confident with. He knew where to skate during the breakout, and he knew killing penalties would be all about hustle.

With twelve players for their game Friday, the Wildcats had to change their strategy quickly before playing the North Park Panthers. Coach put Carter and Chad as centres on the two forward lines. Paul was the seventh forward. He'd play right wing whenever someone needed rest, and he'd get some time on specialty teams.

"I want you on the right side so you can use that big shot," Coach said after practice. "I think this way when you shoot, you'll have plenty of targets to choose from."

There would be just four defencemen, not the usual six. The Wildcats would have to play strong defence and try to get the Panthers to take penalties. Goaltending would be their biggest advantage. Despite all his joking, Jayson was the best in the six-team league, and he would probably see lots of shots.

Paul arrived home exhausted. It was barely 8:30 p.m., but he was going to bed anyway. He took the stairs down to his apartment slowly because his legs burned. To his surprise, his mom came out of her room, holding a book.

"You're home," Paul said. "I thought you were working until nine."

"Two practices in three days? You must be tired," she answered.

He flopped into a chair. "Yeah."

"You should eat and then go to bed. Do you have any homework?"

He did. He dragged himself off the chair and went to the kitchen table with his math and spelling homework. He took roasted chicken and pasta from the fridge and ate straight from the container.

"Want me to microwave that for you?"

Paul looked up as he tried to bring a mouthful of spaghetti in for a landing.

"Nah, I'm okay, thanks. It's good cold."

His mother sat next to him and opened his schoolbooks to have a closer look.

"What are we working on? Ah, math and language arts," she said. "Let's get to work. You know I'm an expert at long division."

For the next thirty minutes, she helped Paul crunch numbers and study word definitions. Five minutes after his homework was finished, Paul was sound asleep.

★★★

The next day at school, Paul and Jayson were told by Mr. Fontaine twice to stop talking about hockey. Paul's first game was the next night, and he asked what Jayson would do if the team lost a faceoff in the defensive zone during a penalty kill. Finally, during recess, Paul pinned Vincent down in the library and quizzed him instead.

Paul produced a notebook with dozens of pages of drawings. Each page had a rink, with the faceoff circles and lines drawn in blue. Paul had written down the drills — as best he could remember them — and the breakout, power play, and penalty kill. There were detailed notes. He had dashed black lines to show how the puck moved. Paul flipped deep into the notebook until he found a page titled "Left-Wing Lock."

"Jayson was not helpful at all," Paul said in a hushed voice. "If we lose the faceoff in our zone during a penalty kill, what should I do?"

"Pray," Vincent said.

Paul looked at him like he was joking. "That's not a good option."

"It's the best option," Vincent said. "We don't like to lose faceoffs when we kill penalties. It never ends well."

After a stern look from the librarian, they moved further back in the library where they could talk a bit louder. Paul wanted to know more about the different options he had depending on where the puck was on the ice.

"If we lose the faceoff in their zone, should I skate to the far boards and look for a quick turnover, or should I retreat into our zone and cover any forward looking for a stretch pass?"

Vincent took Paul's notebook — it said "Wildcats Playbook" on the cover, with "Do Not Share" and "Private, Keep Out" written in thick, black letters. Paul had drawn a big padlock next to a skull-and-crossbones pirate flag.

Vincent thumbed through the pages, stopping to read every so often. Then he started over and looked through the book again.

"This is awesome," he said. "We should make copies. Nobody on our team takes the plays this seriously. Most of us just play hockey without thinking much about systems."

"That's because you guys have all played for a long time," Paul said as he peeked over his shoulder, looking for the librarian.

"You'll be fine," Vincent said. "The fact you even know to ask those questions tells me you understand more than half the players on our team."

Paul kept asking Jayson and Vincent questions for the rest of that day, and all day on Friday, game day

"Are you coming to the game?" he asked Vincent.

He had been in school a few days, and seemed to be recovering well from his concussion.

"Nah, I can't tonight," Vincent said. "I still get pretty tired after school, and this is an away game."

Paul was disappointed. He thought that having Vincent around, even if it was just in the stands or behind the bench, would give him the confidence to make it through his first game.

"Hey, if it makes you feel any better," Vincent said, "I get worried sick before every game."

Paul shot Vincent an uncertain look. "I don't believe you."

"I'm serious," Vincent said. "Probably most of the guys do. You're not the only one worried about falling flat on your back. No matter how many games I've played, I still get that feeling."

Paul could feel his face get red. He couldn't believe someone had told Vincent he had fallen at the first practice. Still, he appreciated the vote of confidence. "Hey," Vincent said as the two best friends went their separate ways. "Good luck. Have fun, and don't worry about the score. Just relax. Really."

Paul kept repeating that as he gathered up his equipment and had a quick bite to eat after school. He even did homework to help him think about something else. Soon, though, it was 5:45 and Coach was knocking at his door. Paul grabbed his hockey bag and two sticks, and headed to the car where Carter waited with the trunk open.

"Here, let me stash that for you," Carter said. "Hope you're ready. I am."

"I'm ready," Paul answered, but his voice felt weak. A part of him wanted to crawl back inside his house and hide under his bedcovers.

"Here, I have something for you," Carter said after they started their drive to the rink.

He tossed a red-and-blue Wildcats jersey to Paul in the back seat. Paul grabbed it and held it up to see the team's logo: a snarling bobcat with a broken hockey stick between its jaws. He turned it over to see the number 22.

"I hope the number is okay," Coach said from the driver's seat. "It was the first one I grabbed off the pile on our way out."

Paul just stared at the sweater in amazement. It was his first real hockey jersey.

"It's perfect. Thank you."

The ride to the rink seemed to last forever. Paul wanted to get there as early as possible. After they arrived and found their dressing room, Paul changed quickly. Just as fast, though, he realized he had put his elbow pads on too early when his shoulder pads wouldn't fit properly. He wasn't concentrating.

He looked around at the faces of the boys who were all now teammates, even though he had only known them a few days. A week ago, he had been skating alone, at night, at Wilden Park. Now, here he was getting geared up for a real game. After a quick pep talk from the coach, they were ready for warm-ups. The Wildcats stood in a line at the door, chatting and shouting encouragement. Most of them were, anyway.

"Here we go, rookie. Don't let us down," Chad said as they hustled onto the ice.

The parents in the small crowd clapped and shouted. There was no loud music or spotlights, but Paul was just as excited. They skated through a few quick warm-up drills before assembling at the bench. Paul stole a look at the other team: there seemed to be hundreds of them, all forming neat lines in their all-black uniforms with roaring yellow Panther logos.

"Don't underestimate these guys," Coach said as they huddled before the opening faceoff. "They're in last place and they're missing some guys, too. But this is their barn. Remember what we said: short shifts, discipline, and defence."

Paul ran it over in his head three times: *discipline and defence*, like they were the most important words in the world.

11 FUN AND GAMES

Paul had no time to worry about how good he was or how well he fit into the team. Two minutes after the opening faceoff, he jumped over the boards for his first shift with the Wildcats. It was a quick change on the fly. He played right wing with Carter at centre and Nathan on the left. The puck was along the left-wing boards in the Panthers' zone. Nathan and Carter battled against the Panthers' top line for possession. The Panthers hadn't changed, and the Wildcats were fresh.

That gave Nathan an advantage. He knifed between a forward and defender to collect the loose puck along the boards. He slid a backhand pass between his legs to Carter, who had to get rid of it quickly — or lose it to a defender. He found Matthew at the point. The big defenceman snapped a quick shot on net, forcing a left-pad save from the Panther goalie. The rebound skidded into the corner boards in front of Paul.

He gave chase, bearing down on a Panthers' defenceman.

Yes, this is my chance, Paul thought.

He had plenty of nervous energy, and he skated hard at his opponent. But the puck skipped past him and out of the zone. Paul realized his mistake. Had he cut off the boards, he might have forced a turnover. Instead, the Panthers gained the red line and dumped the puck into the Wildcats' zone.

Paul promised himself he wouldn't make that mistake again. He charged back into his own zone. Paul moved to his position just above the right faceoff circle. Matthew had the puck to the goalie's left. He pushed it ahead to Nathan, who spotted Carter in the centre, and the Wildcats were back in the other direction.

Paul waited for Carter to dump it in again. Now he was ready to forecheck. The puck was behind the Panther net, so Paul barrelled into the zone, looking to create a turnover. Again he was a second too late and watched the puck scoot under his stick to a wide-open Panther in the corner.

He chased that man next, but the Panthers did a good job of moving the puck. Paul felt like a puppy dog chasing a tennis ball. He huffed and puffed his way to the bench.

"I like your hustle," Coach said behind him. "But if you don't pace yourself, you're not going to last until the first period is over. Think about where the play is going, not where the puck is. Anticipate."

Paul grabbed a bottle and squeezed a jet of water

into his mouth. He felt better. The nervous energy had disappeared. He felt like he was ready for his next shift. It came just a few seconds later, and it ended the same way. Paul spent the first eight or nine minutes of the game skating up and down the right wing.

As the game wore on, though, Paul got his chance. He helped his team cycle the puck in the Panther zone, then found his position on the right wing. Nathan spotted him with a great pass, and all Paul had to do was swing away.

Whoosh!

Paul missed completely when the puck hit a bump and skidded behind him. He banged his stick in frustration as he skated to the bench for a change. He sat watching the next few minutes, trying to understand why he'd barely touched the puck.

Paul searched the ice for an answer.

It wasn't the Panthers. They had fancy uniforms, and lots of players, but they weren't as good as the Wildcats. Paul looked over at the Wildcats' bench as the referee called players to the faceoff. They were smiling and laughing, joking and . . .

"That's it!" he shouted.

Carter looked over at Paul. "What's it?"

Paul could feel his face flush. He hadn't meant to shout out loud, and now everyone on the bench was looking at him.

"Oh, I just figured out a math problem."

Carter laughed. "You're thinking about math? That's messed up, but as long as you're having fun."

Exactly, Paul thought. This should be fun, just like those nights at Wilden Park. Paul realized there was nothing wrong with what he was doing on the ice. He just needed to remind himself of what Vincent had said: relax, have fun, and don't worry about the score. He was doing fine.

As the play restarted, Paul decided he wasn't going to force anything. He was thinking too much. Plays, schemes, and diagrams were swirling in his head. He hadn't taken any time to enjoy himself. He was playing hockey — real hockey — with a great bunch of guys on a Friday night.

In the dressing room before the game, some of the guys had talked about having a sleepover and ordering pizza. They'd watch a movie, stay up too late, and probably drink too much pop. Carter said they could do it at his place because his sisters were both away at tournaments with his mom. Paul would be guest of honour.

As the play zoomed past him again, a big smile spread across his face. The thought of hanging out at Carter's place put Paul in a great mood.

"Okay, Carter, let's get your guys going!" Coach yelled to their line.

Paul put one leg over the bench, waiting for his change. When it came, he felt like he was floating instead of skating. He landed softly on his blades and immediately sprinted into the Panther zone, where their goalie was playing the dump-in from the left corner. He was far out of his crease, and shot the puck behind his net to a defenceman on the right side. Paul reacted quickly and pounced on the player, who had to get rid of the puck quickly. That's when Carter appeared. He intercepted the pass, and spotted Nathan alone in the slot.

Nathan fired the pass into the back of the net.

"Oh, yes!" Paul shouted. "Nice pass, Carter! Great shot, Nathan!"

"That was a great play, Paul!" Carter said as they huddled on the ice to celebrate.

The five players turned and skated toward their bench to trade fist bumps with the team.

"Nice job, Paul!" Coach shouted as they approached. "You started that one."

It was 1–0 for the Wildcats with seven minutes left in the first period. Yet, as the game continued, the shorthanded Wildcats just couldn't keep pace, and it ended at 4–4.

"We were better than them," Paul said to Carter as he pulled his gear from the trunk after the game. "But there just weren't enough of us."

12 WIN AND YOU'RE IN

Exactly one month after he had played his first game with the Wildcats, Paul woke up wondering what it would take to win just once. Since tying the Panthers, they'd lost four straight and fallen to fifth place from first. Paul was amazed at how much he had improved. He was skating better and had four assists, but the team was still losing.

Now the Wildcats needed a win to reach the play-offs. In a six-team league, the top four teams played a semifinal while the two bottom teams played a consolation round. At least some of the Wildcats were getting healthier. They would have nearly a full roster for the last game against the first-place Mount Royal Bulldogs.

The only thing missing was their star player, Vincent. He had been free of his symptoms for more than a week. He expected to be back for the last practice before playoffs as long as the team could beat the Bulldogs.

That was all Paul could think about as he arrived at

the rink: win for Vincent. He was re-taping his hockey stick when the door opened and Chad walked into the dressing room. He looked up at the whiteboard with the team lineup on it, and sneered.

"Oh, come on," Chad said. "Your number shouldn't even be on that board, rookie."

Paul was confused. His number 22 was on the third line and the penalty-killing unit, like always. Chad threw his equipment into a corner. He banged his stick on the floor as he walked to the centre of the room. He yelled at Jayson to stop the music blaring from the portable speakers he had connected to his iPod.

"You guys want to win this game, right?" Chad asked in a stern voice.

Most of the Wildcats avoided looking him in the eye, so he answered for them.

"Of course you do. That's why we need to get back to our old team."

Chad pointed a finger at Paul. "We didn't start losing until the rookie got here."

Chad waited, but nobody said anything. He threw his stick at his equipment. "It's time for him to go," Chad said.

Normally full of laughter, the Wildcats' dressing room was as quiet as a church on Sunday. Everyone looked at Paul, who would have crawled into his hockey bag if it hadn't smelled so bad. He stopped lacing his skates and braced for Chad's next outburst. He thought about getting up and leaving his gear behind. It wasn't his, anyway. He was about to stand when he heard another voice.

"Sit down, Chad," Matthew boomed in a voice that made him sound ten years older. "You're being such a jerk!"

Everyone turned to Matthew. Paul's heart skipped a beat, and then he heard a third voice. It was his. "Wait, this is my fight."

Before he could think twice, Paul stood. His voice sounded so weak, he barely recognized it.

"I've had enough people fight my battles for me," Paul said. "This isn't just your team, Chad. I was asked here. I think I've proven myself. I'm sorry if I had to borrow equipment, or that I might look a little different than you, but I can't do anything about that. Oh, and my dad is from Trinidad, not Jamaica or the Bahamas."

Paul looked around the room. "Tell you what, Chad. Let's have that vote you wanted before. If the rest of the guys feel the same way as you, I'll quit. You guys want me to go?"

Nobody said anything, not even Chad. The door creaked open, and Coach walked into the room.

"Everything okay in here?"

"You bet, Coach," Matthew said. "We were just giving the team a pep talk."

Paul didn't think Coach would buy it.

"Good idea," Coach said as he surveyed the team. "Any questions?"

More silence. Coach looked slowly around the room. Most of the players stared down at their skates.

Paul felt like he was standing on stage for a school play, but he'd forgotten his lines. He started to sweat. He could hear his heart beating.

"Good," Coach said. "Get dressed. We've got a game to win."

The players jumped up and cheered. They screamed out "Yeah!" together. Jayson turned the music back on full blast. Chad walked back to his hockey bag and didn't say anything.

Paul's legs were so wobbly he was afraid he would fall. He had thought he was about to lose his place on the team, but now the Wildcats seemed more united than ever. Paul went back to his borrowed hockey bag, put on the rest of his borrowed equipment, and breathed a huge sigh of relief. He grabbed his stick and turned to his teammates.

"Let's go to work!" he shouted, and they roared in return and banged him on the shoulder.

The team nearly sprinted out to the ice. It was another away game, and the Bulldogs had the noisiest rink in the league. Still, Paul was surprised when he heard fans clapping and cheering, and music blasting from loudspeakers.

As they emerged from the dressing room, Paul

spotted a familiar face. Tracey Evans was there with two of her teammates from the triple-A girls' team, the Saskatoon Swift. They hung over the railing, giving high-fives to the guys as they took the ice.

"Not bad for peewee house league!" she shouted to Paul.

The team took their newfound determination into the first period and jumped all over the Bulldogs for a quick 2–0 lead, thanks to goals from Carter and Matt. Paul was more relieved than happy. He was playing on a line with Derrick and Nathan, but they had trouble finding a groove.

He had hoped it wouldn't matter much, with many of the veteran Wildcats playing well, but he was wrong. As good as the team was in the first period, they were just as bad in the second. Everything fell apart and the Bulldogs tied the game with what seemed to Paul like little effort.

"Let's get it together," Coach said on the bench. "We've stopped moving our feet, and guess what? We're taking all the penalties. Start skating and good things will happen."

Coach's scolding worked.

Once the Bulldogs pulled even they relaxed. Meanwhile, the Wildcats took it as motivation. Paul's line was better, too. The Bulldogs' defencemen had no time to make good plays with Paul in pursuit. Derrick was there to intercept bad passes, and Nathan had three great chances on net.

The only thing missing was the goal, and the second period ended 2–2.

"You guys are playing awesome!" Tracey shouted to Paul as he came off the ice. "Try faking a shot, and then go top shelf. This goalie goes down too quick."

Paul smiled. "Thanks!"

The Wildcats kept buzzing the Bulldogs in the third period and were outshooting them 28 to 19 with eight minutes to play. It was then Paul found himself checking an opposing defenceman at the Wildcats' blue line. Paul surprised the player, knocked loose the puck, and started to skate away with it.

Instead of letting Paul get a breakaway, the defenceman hooked him from behind. Paul pumped his legs hard but fell to the ice. Everyone on the Wildcats' bench jumped into the air shouting, "Penalty!"

"Two minutes for hooking," the referee said as he skated past them.

Paul, Derrick, and Nathan skated toward the bench, expecting the power-play unit to take over for them. Instead, Coach waved Paul's line back onto the ice.

"Keep doing what you're doing," Coach shouted at them. "Don't change a thing."

Derrick won the faceoff back to Cody on defence. It went across to Nathan, who gained centre ice and dumped it into the corner.

"What are they doing? That's not our power play!" Chad shouted.

That was Paul's chance. He timed it perfectly and pounced on a defenceman who was trying to clear the puck. Paul extended his stick to block the pass and heard an awful *cracking* sound. He looked down to see his stick in two pieces. He dropped it so he wouldn't get a penalty for using broken equipment and charged back to his bench so someone could replace him.

As he approached the bench, he heard Coach yelling: "Stick! Lefty!"

Without breaking stride, Paul grabbed a stick that appeared from the bench for him and skated back into the zone. The Wildcats still had possession of the puck. The Bulldogs hadn't noticed his return, and Paul settled unguarded into the right faceoff circle. The Wildcats cycled down low before sending it back to Cody at the point. The defenceman zipped it to the open right-winger: Paul.

The saucer pass was perfect. Cody rolled the puck off his stick so that it was high enough to get over a diving defender. It spun in the air like a flying saucer, and settled perfectly for Paul. He stopped it, faked a shot, and watched the goalie spill onto the ice. Paul wound up and slammed a shot so hard he dropped to one knee to keep his balance. For an instant there was nothing. When Paul looked up all he could see were his four teammates skating hard toward him. They mobbed him. Everything felt like it was in slow motion.

"Yeah! Amazing!" someone yelled at Paul from the pile of teammates above him. "Nice goal, rookie!"

He skated to the bench, exhausted, and stunned that he had scored. He spotted Tracey sitting in seats above their bench and shouted, "Good advice!"

He plunked himself down and looked at the stick in his hands: Thunderbolt.

"Whose stick is this?" he called to his teammates.

"Mine," a voice from the middle of the bench said, "and I need it back."

Paul looked over, and gulped. He handed the black-and-red stick back to its owner.

"Oh. Thanks, Chad."

13 THE FINAL COUNTDOWN

Paul pushed open the dressing-room door. It slammed against the concrete wall. He couldn't contain his excitement. It was the playoffs, and the Wildcats were a whole team again. They were fresh off a 4–2 win against the Bulldogs. Paul's first goal of the season was the winner. He spotted Vincent in the far corner. This was the first time Paul had the chance to play with his best friend, who had finally recovered from his concussion.

"Hey, Vincent," Paul said happily. "You ready to do this? I'm so pumped."

"You bet," Vincent said.

Paul sensed something was wrong as he sat down. "You better not have a headache."

Vincent motioned toward the whiteboard with the team lineup. Paul's number 22 was now on the fourth line instead of the third. With Vincent back on the team, everyone would have to take a lesser role.

"You should be on the second line, not me,"

Vincent said. "You're the reason we beat the Bulldogs, and I'm so out of shape."

Paul stopped his friend.

"Don't worry about it," Paul said as he unzipped his hockey bag. "I'm just glad you guys are all back. This is going to be fun."

After the players got dressed, Carter called everyone together.

"Paul, come here. It's your turn to do this."

He asked Paul to stand at the door. As the Wildcats headed for the ice, they each gave him a fist bump. The team filed onto the ice as a complete unit for the first time in more than a month.

Carter gathered them for a team cheer: "Three, two, one: Let's go Wild!"

The players shouted back "Cats!" and pumped their fists.

They started the first game of the playoffs against the Stonebridge Phantoms like they were playing for the Stanley Cup. Vincent, Carter, and Rudy played on the first line, and helped the Wildcats jump out to a 3–1 lead after two periods. They passed like pros, darting across the blue line like fighter jets. But the Phantoms started to play better in the third and threatened to score many times. If it wasn't for Jayson in goal, the game might have been much closer.

The next goal would be critical.

"Come on, Vincent!" Paul shouted from the bench

as the top line mounted a renewed attack.

Carter charged up the middle of the ice, snapping a hard pass to Vincent on the right side, and the trio burst into the Phantom zone. Vincent ripped a hard pass along the boards behind the net. Rudy, on left wing, let it slip to Matt at the point.

The Phantoms didn't know where to turn.

Matthew hit Vincent at the right post with a pass. Vincent faked and passed to Carter, alone in the slot. He tapped it into the net for a 4–1 lead. The Wildcats on the bench were all standing, watching the display. They threw their arms into the air as Carter scored.

"Yeah!" Paul yelled from the bench as he high-fived Derrick. "That was amazing passing. They looked just like the pros!"

The Wildcats rolled to a 5–1 win. They played even better in their next game, and gave Jayson a 4–0 shut-out. It put them into the championship series against their archrivals, the Bulldogs. With their sweep in the best-of-three series, it meant the players had a whole Saturday night free. Some of the guys got together for a movie night, and others went to watch the Blades play the Regina Pats in a Western Hockey League game. Paul thanked his teammates for inviting him, but he had something important to do.

★★★

Paul dumped a bag of pucks onto the ice at Wilden Park and started shooting, slowly. He had only one stick left and didn't want to break it. As he swung, he started to get angry. He wanted to shoot harder. He wanted to buy new sticks. Vincent had said he could borrow one, but Paul was sick of not having his own equipment.

"You missed the last two," someone said.

Paul jumped. "Chad, what are you doing here?" He was suddenly nervous.

"I decided I needed some extra practice. I missed my last three open shots. I haven't scored in a while."

"Take a few," Paul said, relieved but suspicious.

Chad hopped over the boards. He reached back and grabbed two Thunderbolts.

"I don't get it," Chad said as he slid toward Paul. "Why do you come out here at night? You can't see a thing. And it's cold."

Paul fidgeted with the pucks on the ice. He was embarrassed to admit he still didn't think he was good enough to play on the team. The playoffs were different. He wanted to make sure he was ready.

"I get to shoot as much as I like, and it's not that cold," he said instead. "You should be here in January."

Paul shoved half his pucks to Chad, who gave Paul his extra stick to hold. Chad lined up the pucks like he was in a skills competition. Five shots, five misses. The pucks were all over the rink. One flew into a deep snowbank over the boards.

"We'll need a flashlight to find that one," Paul said, laughing.

Chad smiled. "I don't think we'll find it until June."

Paul went next, dropping his wooden stick for a Thunderbolt. He held it out and looked at Chad. "Can I use it? I won't break it, I promise."

Chad nodded but quickly held out his hand to stop Paul from shooting.

"Wait. We take five shots each. If you score more, you keep it."

Paul smiled. He liked that idea, but had a question. "What if you win?"

"Then you quit the Wildcats," Chad answered.

Paul looked quickly at Chad again. He was standing there with a grin on his face. Paul wasn't sure if he was serious, but he agreed anyway. Even if he was kidding, this was Paul's chance to prove to Chad that he deserved a place on the team.

Paul stood over the first puck and gripped the Thunderbolt. He had almost forgotten how light it felt. Paul drew up the stick and followed through with a nice, smooth stroke. The blade scraped off the ice and sent the puck whizzing at the net.

Thud!

It hit the boards. Paul looked at his missed shot for a second. His breath froze in a cloud above his head as he took a deep breath.

"Nervous?" Chad asked.

"Nah." Paul reset himself. With four more swings he scored four straight. They weren't as hard as Chad's, but they spun straight. Three found the back of the net, and one pinged off the bar and into the net.

"How do you see the goal?" Chad asked. "Maybe I need glasses. I can't see a thing."

Paul could sense Chad's frustration. He felt bad for him, but also proud that he was better at something than his more experienced teammate.

"I think you're psyching yourself out. The street lights are pretty bright. I know where the posts are, and I just aim there. Usually they go in, but not always."

Paul watched Chad take a deep breath, wind up, and fire.

Ping!

The puck hit the crossbar so hard the net jumped. Two more pucks hit the boards behind the net.

"I still don't get it," Chad said.

Paul grabbed one of the pucks and fired an easy wrist shot that landed softly in the net.

"I'm here a lot, plus I forget that it's dark and cold. Maybe you're thinking too much."

Chad collected another puck. Paul could see he was concentrating. He slammed a puck hard off the corner where the back post attached to the top of the net. It was a nearly perfect shot.

"Awesome!" Paul said. "But Vincent taught me something playing Xbox at his house. I think your stick is too high, so it takes you too long to shoot. It's like you're holding down the 'X' button too long. It's better to be more accurate."

"Xbox, eh?" Chad said. "Okay."

They walked to the net and retrieved the pucks, then brought them back to their spot.

"You don't need practice," Paul said. "You have an amazing shot. I'm sure you'll score soon."

"We all need practice," Chad said. "I've been watching you in games. You seem to always get your shots on net."

Paul began to feel more at ease. "Thanks. I wish I was as tough as you. Nobody likes it when you stand in front of their net."

Chad shrugged his shoulders. "You think so? My dad says I still need to be tougher, though. He says if I don't score, I'll never make rep next year."

Paul watched as Chad shot four more, scoring three times. He flashed a satisfied grin. It was one of the few times Paul could remember him smiling lately. It gave Paul some confidence.

"I have to ask you," Paul said, pausing as he thought about the best way to say it. ". . . How come you don't want me on the team?"

Chad gathered up the last puck for a shot. He moved it back and forth but didn't shoot.

"I dunno," he said. "Well, I was kinda mad you got to join and pay less, plus you got all that coaching. My dad said everyone should be treated the same. But I had no idea you would even come outside to practise. I'm not really mad anymore. And you're helping the team."

Chad passed Paul his second Thunderbolt and turned to walk away. Paul held both sticks across his arms like they were priceless treasures. "Wait, these are yours."

Chad turned and looked back at Paul. "We had a deal, and you beat me twice. I guess that means you get two sticks."

Something suddenly became clear to Paul. "You didn't come here to practise, did you?"

Chad was halfway over the boards.

"Um . . . not really, I guess. My dad and I drove past on our way to the Blades game. He laughed and said you needed all the practice you could get," Chad said as he jumped the rest of the way over the boards. "It made me mad, so I told him to take me home. I'm tired of his complaining. He always yells at the refs, too. Hockey's not fun anymore. I came here to find out why you're always so happy and positive."

Paul felt a bit embarrassed, like he had just over-heard a personal conversation.

"Oh. Um, hey, thanks again," Paul said. "I'm glad you came out. I had fun."

14 PLAYOFF HOCKEY

Paul arrived at the Mount Royal arena ninety minutes before the final game of the best-of-three championship series. His mother dropped him off, wished him good luck, and went grocery shopping. She promised to return for the start of the game. It would be the first time Paul's mom had seen him play. She said she was more nervous than he was. Paul didn't believe her.

"Mom, I feel like I'm going to fall over," Paul said as he pulled the hockey bag from the car. "My legs are all wobbly."

She gave him that sympathetic, motherly smile. "You'll do great. At least you get to play. All I can do is watch. That's a helpless feeling."

Paul shut the trunk, grabbed his hockey bag, and headed into the rink, feeling good about the game. The series had been intense so far. The Mount Royal Bulldogs won the first game 3–1. They had scored an empty-net goal in the final minute. The Wildcats played their best hockey of the season in Game 2.

They clawed back into the series with a 2–1 victory. Paul couldn't believe how amazing Jayson had been in net. Vincent scored both goals for the Wildcats on the power play.

"That's how we're going to win this thing," Coach had shouted excitedly after the game. "Discipline and hard work!"

Paul cheered along with the rest of his teammates even though sometimes he felt like a fan with really good seats. He had played a few shifts each period and had even helped kill penalties. If that was what the team needed in the third game, then that was what he was determined to do, Paul thought. Paul looked at the bulletin board in the arena lobby. It said "Wildcats, Room No. 5." He walked down the hallway and found the room. Paul dropped his hockey bag outside the door and pushed on it with both hands. It was locked. He was the first to arrive.

"You're here early," Coach said as he emerged around another corner a few minutes later.

"I don't like being late," Paul said.

"That's a good quality to have, Paul. Hey, let's talk for a second."

Coach warmed his hands around a cup of coffee as they watched kids from the figure skating club practise their jumps and spins on the ice.

"I hope you're having fun, Paul."

Paul looked up, surprised. "Yeah, this is amazing.

I wish I could have started at the beginning of the season."

Coach smiled. "Me too, but I'm glad you found us. If it's okay with your mom, you should apply for Jump Start next season. Every August we have an equipment swap, too. There's always lots of good stuff for cheap."

Paul nodded his head. "For sure. I'll totally do that."

"But let's not think about that now," Coach continued. "I need you to be ready today. Anything could happen. I've been watching that other team closely. I think we can beat them today, and I think I know how."

Paul didn't have time to think about what Coach meant.

"Let's go Wild!" Carter shouted as he walked down the hallway.

"Cats!" Paul yelled, and their screams echoed through the nearly empty rink.

Carter shook a bottle of a bright purple sports drink as he arrived outside the room. He gave Paul a high-five as the rink attendant unlocked the dressing-room door. They found their places in the room and started to get ready. Slowly, the rest of the Wildcats filtered into the arena. The guys were upbeat but on edge. The winner of this game would claim the trophy, and the Bulldogs had home-ice advantage.

As the players started to get dressed, Coach opened the door and took out his lineup sheet. He took a blue marker from the ledge of the whiteboard and wrote out his lines. Paul, as he expected, found his number 22 on the fourth line and penalty-killing unit.

The first period was as close as Paul had expected. He played a handful of shifts, helping the Wildcats kill Chad's roughing penalty. Paul was at his best skating hard at the defence, keeping them off balance. His line with Derrick and Nathan was on the ice more than usual and had some good chances. The Bulldogs scored first, but Carter scored for the Wildcats eight minutes later. The goaltenders took control after that, and the first period ended in a 1–1 tie.

The players were sitting in the dressing room after the first period, checking their sticks or drying their gloves when Coach walked in and called them to attention.

"Derrick, Nathan, Paul: you're doing great. They have some good players on that other bench, but we're deeper. You guys might be the difference."

Paul bumped fists with Derrick and Nathan as they stood for the second period. It wasn't long before they had their first shift. Paul loved being first into the other team's zone on dump-ins, and he got the chance to chase the puck early.

Derrick won a faceoff in the neutral zone, and instead of pulling it back to the defenceman, he pushed it between the other centre's legs and charged ahead. Paul banged his stick on the ice as the signal for Derrick to dump the puck into the Bulldogs' zone.

"C'mon boys, you can do this!" Paul heard Vincent yell from the bench.

Paul felt like nothing could stop him. His speed caused the Bulldogs' defenceman to blindly swing away at the puck in hopes of clearing the zone. Instead, it went straight to Nathan at the left wing. He came in off the boards and snapped a quick shot on net. The Bulldogs' goalie kicked his left pad out but gave up a huge rebound. Paul couldn't believe his eyes. The puck came straight for him. He stepped into a hard slapshot and slammed it home for a 2–1 lead early in the second period.

All Paul could hear was yelling and screaming. Parents shouted, blew their plastic horns, or rang their bells. Paul raised his arms and jumped as high as he could before he was bowled over by his celebrating teammates. He barely had time to catch a glimpse of his mom in the stands hugging the woman beside her.

"Wicked! Just wicked!" Vincent said as he head-butted Paul's helmet when he returned to the bench.

"Careful, don't hurt yourself. I can't score all the goals!"

The Bulldogs wilted after that. They were barely hanging on when the horn sounded to end the second period. There were more congratulations for Paul's line in the dressing room and the promise of even more ice time in the third period. Derrick, Nathan, and Paul sat together. They didn't take off their jerseys to cool off, and took only short swigs of water. They couldn't wait to get back on the ice.

"Don't let up now," Vincent told them. "This is where we win this thing."

Vincent's leadership carried from the dressing room onto the ice for the third period. He was a one-man highlight reel — spinning and passing, shooting and playing solid defence. He even drew a quick penalty. Yet, no matter how hard the Wildcats worked, they just couldn't beat the Bulldogs' goalie.

"Why can't we score?" Paul asked Derrick, beside him.

Paul looked back in time to see Vincent battling for the puck along the far boards. He was tied up with another winger when a Bulldogs' defenceman charged into the play, looking for the loose puck. Instead, he caught Vincent with his head down. The collision lifted the Wildcats' star off his feet and sent him flying back onto the ice.

He didn't move right away, and the referee immediately blew his whistle. Everyone went silent as Coach shuffled across the ice holding the ref's arm for balance. Coach bent down to check on Vincent, and they stayed there for a few seconds. Finally, Vincent sat up and the fans clapped. Paul didn't think he was hurt that badly as they arrived back at the bench. Vincent didn't stop, though. His dad was waiting for him, and they went into the dressing room.

Coach turned back to the ref.

"You can't let that one go," he said. "It was a high hit."

The ref shook his head. "It wasn't pretty, but they just ran into each other."

"No way," Coach continued.

As the other Wildcats watched the exchange, Paul stared back at the hall. He kept hoping to see Vincent re-emerge from the dressing room, but he never did.

With ten minutes to play and the championship in the balance, the Wildcats suddenly had a big hole to fill. With Vincent out of the lineup, the Bulldogs scored two goals in three minutes for a 3–2 lead. The Wildcats were scattered and made too many mistakes. Chad took another roughing penalty. He skated up to the Bulldogs' defenceman, who knocked Vincent out of the game and cross-checked him.

It forced the Wildcats to kill a penalty with just five minutes to play. Then, with ninety seconds on the clock and fans from both teams standing and cheering, Coach walked down the bench and tapped Paul on the shoulder.

"You're the extra attacker when Jayson comes to the bench," he said. "Find some empty space, and shoot as hard as you can. Just get it on net."

The Bulldogs barely paid attention to Paul when he finally hit the ice. They were too busy worrying about Chad in front of the net, and Matthew running the point.

Paul settled into a soft spot in the Bulldogs' zone. Matthew faked a shot, which froze the defenders and goalie. The puck came skidding across to Paul, but he barely had enough time to shoot before a Bulldogs' forward banged into him.

The goalie made a glove save but dropped the puck. The Wildcats stormed the net looking for a rebound. Chad jammed at it as a crowd of players collapsed around the crease. The Wildcats on the ice shouted at the referee, saying the puck was in the net.

"It's in! It's in!" Chad and Carter screamed together.

But the horn sounded, and the ref blew his whistle. "After the horn, boys," the ref said.

The Bulldogs on the bench poured over the boards and mobbed their goalie. Paul, still on his knees, looked up at the scoreboard: DOGS 3, CATS 2.

15 POST-GAME REACTION

Paul pressed the Shoot button just long enough, aimed with the joystick, and pulled the trigger. The puck whizzed past the Colorado Avalanche goalie.

"Yeah! Overtime winner for the Oilers!"

Vincent dropped his controller. "Oh, now you score," he laughed. "Where was that yesterday?"

"At least I was on the ice."

Vincent and Paul sat on the floor, controllers in hand. They hooted with laughter. The Xbox was set up in Vincent's room again, and a silver medal hung from his dresser mirror. Paul was getting ready for the seventh and deciding game of their Xbox Stanley Cup, but Vincent stared at the medal.

"Silver. I can't believe it. We were so close."

Paul was confused. He was focused on the Xbox.

"Oh, yeah, that's awesome. We won second. I'm never going to take mine off," Paul said as he raised his silver medal from around his neck.

He let it drop again and flipped through the menu

to start the next game. "Hey, are we playing, or do you have another concussion?"

"Oh, thanks for that. I keep telling you I didn't get another concussion," Vincent said as he picked up his controller again. "You just have to be careful. When you get one concussion, it's easier to get a second. I told my dad to let me play, but he said it was better to be safe."

Paul pressed the Pause button. "Yeah, I know. I'm just teasing. Believe me, we were glad to see you in the dressing room after the game. I thought we might have to drive to the hospital to visit you. I'll just never know how that hit wasn't a penalty."

Rock music poured from Vincent's TV as the game started. They stared straight ahead.

"You know I never get penalties called for me. I guess the refs just think I'm too good."

"Ha!" Paul bumped Vincent with his shoulder just as one of his Oilers flattened one of Vincent's players.

"Hey, no fair!" Vincent bumped back, and they swayed back and forth, the whole time keeping firm hold of their controllers.

Paul finally shuffled a safe distance away. They mashed buttons and trash talked, and in the end Vincent's team prevailed 5–4. "Champion!" he shouted.

"When did you get so good at this?" Paul asked in disbelief. "I bet you didn't have a concussion. I bet you were just at home practising to beat me."

"You wish, dude. I was always better than you."

Post-Game Reaction

Paul stood up and stretched. He had slept on a foam mattress in Vincent's bedroom.

"I better get going. My mom traded shifts so she could watch our game. She should be home soon, and I should be there. I have to start preparing her for next season."

Vincent stood up too, grabbing his back. "Oh, man, I think I slept on my controller last night. See you at school tomorrow."

Paul walked the short couple of blocks back home to find his mom had already made breakfast. Eggs, pancakes, and fresh fruit were on the table when he arrived.

"Oh, good, you're home."

Paul said hi, kissed her on the cheek and flumped into his chair. Without saying much more he immediately started inhaling everything within his reach.

"Oh, thanks, Mom. This is amazing. I'm so hungry."

"That was some game," she said. "You are so good. I was so proud of you. I sat beside Rudy's mother. She said you were one of the best players at the end."

Paul shovelled another pancake onto his plate, slapped a slab of butter on top, and drenched it in maple syrup.

"Really, she said that? Yeah, I don't know. I still have lots to learn."

There was nothing left on the table by the time Paul was finished eating. He groaned as he put the milk, juice, butter, and syrup back into the fridge. He picked up a tea towel and started drying dishes while his mom washed.

"So, Mom, how about . . ."

"Next year," she interrupted. "You better get a summer job. Your auntie says you can cut her lawn. I'm sure you could convince the neighbours, too. You'll have to save every penny."

Paul grabbed her in a hug and let out an excited roar.

"You mean it? Oh, thanks, Mom. That's amazing. I'm going to call Vince and Carter."

"Tell them you'll need a ride. I could barely watch that game. My heart can't take all that excitement."

Paul called his friends and told them they should train all summer.

"We need to start running hills at Diefenbaker Park," he suggested.

Carter groaned.

"Don't let my dad hear you say that, or we'll be there every week."

Paul flopped onto the couch, and within minutes of clicking on the TV, was sound asleep. He woke up in time for lunch but spent the rest of the day watching hockey and doing homework.

"I'm zonked," he told his mom. He was back in bed by half past eight.

The next morning at school, Paul sat down at his desk, still rubbing sleep from his eyes. Math was first, but he didn't mind. He gripped the silver medal in his hoodie pocket. Knowing it was there was enough to get him through the day. He kept replaying his final shot in his head. If it had been just an inch lower, he might have scored. He debated and discussed it with Vincent all through lunch hour. Paul was still thinking about it as the final bell rang and he gathered his books and headed outside. Paul had to walk carefully across the melting, sloppy sports field toward the back gate. He was headed home but stopped at the school's outdoor hockey rink first, or what was left of it. He leaned over the boards and watched as the sun reflected off the snowbanks.

Paul used to get miserable when the outdoor rinks thawed, but it was different now. His first season of organized hockey had been exciting but exhausting.

"We just about did it," a voice said from behind him. "If you'd taught me how to shoot sooner, maybe we would've won the playoffs."

Paul laughed. "I could hear you coming from a mile away," he said as Chad approached. "It's hard to sneak up on someone in this muck. And maybe if you had given me that Thunderbolt a little sooner, I would've scored twice as many goals."

Chad stood next to Paul at the boards. "You're right," Chad said. "Not about the stick. But if I'd just offered you my help sooner, we probably would have won more games."

"It's fine," Paul said. "It worked out. You just wanted the best for the team. I get it."

Chad scooped up snow, pressed it into a ball with

his bare hands, and tossed it into the melting ice.

"I bet this ice melts by the end of the day," he said. "And you know what that means? It's almost baseball season. You going to play this summer?"

Paul smiled and stretched out his hand to feel the sun. A chinook had blown over the Rocky Mountains, making it warmer than normal.

"I love baseball. Can I play catcher?"

Chad shoved Paul's shoulder playfully. "No way! That's my position."

The ground was slushy and slippery. They jostled, trying not to fall into any muck.

"Now, boys," Tracey's voice called from nearby. "Don't make me come over there."

Paul looked over at Chad, whose face was as red as ever.

"Don't worry about us," Paul shouted back. "We're all good."

They moved back from the boards and headed for the gate.

"Hey, you know what would be great?" Chad said. "The baseball team should practise at night this summer. That way, when we play games in the daytime, we'd be amazing hitters."

Paul thought Chad was serious until a smile spread across his face.

"Yeah, right," Paul said. "That's just dangerous. You'd have to be crazy to play baseball at night."

ACKNOWLEDGEMENTS

This book would not have been possible without help from the following people: Christie Harkin provided an ideal balance of encouragement and motivation. Ross Freake's early editing put me on the right path. Kat Mototsune's insight helped transform this collection of words into a story. Hannah Bidwell lent invaluable expertise about a young athlete living with a concussion. And thank you to all the staff at Lorimer, and to anyone who has ever shovelled snow off an outdoor ice rink so kids could play hockey.

MARQUIS

Québec, Canada